STORIES WE TELL OUR CHILDREN

Stories We Tell Our Children

—

Marc Nash

LENDAL PRESS

First published in 2021 by Lendal Press
Woodend, The Crescent, Scarborough, YO11 2PW
an imprint of Valley Press · lendalpress.com

ISBN 978-1-912436-94-1
Catalogue no. LP0002

A CIP record is available from the British Library.

Cover and text design by Peter Barnfather
Cover illustration by Ben Hardaker
Edited by Daniel James

Printed and bound in Great Britain by
Imprint Digital, Upton Pyne, Exeter

Seeing comes before words. The child looks
and recognises before it can speak. But there is
also another sense in which seeing comes before
words. It is seeing which establishes our place in
the surrounding world; we explain that world
with words, but words can never undo the fact
that we are surrounded by it. The relation between
what we see and what we know is never settled.

JOHN BERGER

They fuck you up, your mum and dad.
They may not mean to, but they do.

PHILIP LARKIN

In sending the young out into life with such
a false psychological orientation, education is
behaving as though one were to equip people
starting on a Polar expedition with summer
clothing and maps of the Italian Lakes.

SIGMUND FREUD

Swatch With Mother

"What colour is an orange?"

"It's orange silly mummy. Give me a harder one."

It's only orange because they inject it with dye. Because we expect oranges to look, well, orange. "Okay then, what colour is a… tomato?"

"Red!"

Green while still early on the vine, but yes, the judges say they can accept your answer. "Okey-dokey, how about an apple?"

"Green!"

"Aha, but there are also red ones aren't there?" He's nodding, but his expression is pained. Is it perplexing him, or does he just hate to be wrong?

"Not all the apple though. The seeds inside are brown."

"Pips darling. An apple's seeds are called pips." No, he's not perplexed. He just hates to lose then. Wonder who he gets that from? "Very good point though. Isn't it amazing how nature decides the colour of things? Since from those brown pips grows the tree with its brown trunk and branches. But from those brown branches grow green leaves and apples."

"Or red."

"Or red."

"Do another one mummy!"

"What colour is… custard?"

"Yellow! Urgh! I don't like custard!"

"I know you don't poppet. But it still has a colour." But not an innate warning colour, like some poisonous animals cautioning of their toxicity. Not a perilous colour that is, until some human animal prefixes it with a venomous modifier, like 'cowardy custard' in the nursery; or 'yellow chicken' in the school playground; yellowbelly on the army assault course; and yellow star in the concentration camps. Yet there was nothing cowardly about your fight to stay in the world at birth when you were born with jaundice. "What colour is blancmange?" Oooh, that's stumped him. The clue is not in the name, 'white eating'. Is he going to cry? "I'll give you a clue. You've eaten it and it's strawberry flavoured."

"Oooh-oooh, it's pink isn't it? Like a flamingo at the zoo."

"Yes pink! Brilliant. Well done." Surely we've been through the entire spectrum up and down now? No wait, I've missed one. "What colour is chalk?"

"Chalk? What's chalk?"

"Oh yes, you've probably never come across chalk before. What colour are the boards your teachers write on at nursery school?"

"White! They're called whiteboards. Silly mummy, the colour is in the name."

And the colour was ever in the name in my day, when they were blackboards. Even when they were actually green. Green screen behind movie special effects, the acme of all illusion. "You're very good at your colours. So we're –" (we're?) "– going to test you with bit harder ones now. I'm going to say a colour and you're going to give me something that is that colour. Sound good?" He's nodding so enthusiastically I'm afraid his head is going to fall off. He was ripe for a change too then it seems. "You can't give me anything we've already said from before though. Only new things. Okay, here we go then. Give me something that is grey."

"An elephant!"

"Wow! That was really fast!" And yet of all the copious grey skin of that fine, noble beast, the poachers hunt it for its lone outcrop of white. "Give me something that is brown."

"A tree trunk!"

"Ah no, we said nothing we've had already, didn't we?" He slowly nods grudging agreement. Who am I to append such an adjective to his motion, maybe it's axiomatically slow in time with his thought processes. An adverb, that's even worse. Even though they lend colour to our actions. There goes the pursed lower lip. Thinking hard, or a pout? That's stopped him in his tracks. Now he's looking around the room...

"The table!"

Great, I've managed to make it so we're now basically playing a version of 'I-Spy'. "Not all tables are brown."

"That one is. The one the chairs are all around."

"That's because it's made from...?"

"Wood!"

"Correct. And where does wood come from? No...?" Nope. Not got that connection lined up yet. "Wood comes from trees darling. So wooden things are nearly always brown, dark brown or light brown depending on the tree." Unless they've painted it, or it's from Ikea. "Aren't we learning lots of new things today? Another one? Okay. Give me something purple." My late mother's ink colour of preference. Things to do with royalty. Bit abstract though. "That's a hard one darling. Even mummy's struggling with this one."

"That fruit mummy? The one I don't like."

That hardly narrows it down for me. "Which one darling?"

"It's quite small, smaller than an apple or pear. It looks the colour of bruises, all over."

The colour of bruises? Ugh! Where did he get that one from? "Ah I think you mean a plum! Well done, yes the skin of a plum is purple." But not its flesh. "It's a very good example. But it's slightly tricky, because there's also a colour that's called plum, which is a shade of purple. There's quite a few colours that have ever so slightly different shades." Not quite so proficient at your colours now with this little bombshell dropped, are you? "Some of them are named after fruits, like there's a colour 'peach', 'strawberry' is really a colour as well. 'Damson' is a colour that's named after a type of plum –"

"That's really confusing!"

Isn't it just? You wait until you encounter the ambiguous hue that is 'bice', twice the fun of both blue and green. Of course, more interesting are the shades named after gemstones, carmine, ruby, jade, topaz, amethyst... But we probably won't go there today. If only I had one of each in my jewellery box to show you. Unlikely to interest you I suppose. Now if you had a little sister...

"Mum?"

"Yes darling?"

"They're called 'black' grapes, but I'd say they were

more the colour of plums, or purple."

"Yes, I think you're right. They are more purple than black. But what about raisins? You know what raisins are don't you?"

"They're yummy!"

"Ha yes I know they're yummy scrummy! But do you know what fruit they're made from? No? They're made by taking all the water and juice out from black grapes."

"That's weird. Sounds a bit yucky. Why would they do that?"

"But you said you like the taste of raisins?"

"I do."

"So they can't be yucky then, can they? Come on, what colour would you say raisins are?"

"... Black?"

Black indeed, the colour of your father's dark heart. "Yes, again, I'd say you were right. They look black. Yet we know they're made from purple coloured grapes."

"Maybe it's the water and juice that give them their colour?"

Ah, time to move on to the advanced level. "That's an interesting idea. But I think it's more to do with what happens to a grape when it shrinks to make a raisin. It becomes a lot smaller and it's no longer smooth but all wrinkled." As with a mother's skin after birth, which unlike your newborn creases, never smooths back out. "That means the light affects it differently than from when it was a smooth grape." With me so far? "See darling, all colour is light. Light is made up of all the colours in what's called a spectrum. Like a rainbow with all the colours spread out next to each other always in the same order. Because each colour has what is called a different wavelength of light. That of blue is different to that of red. Our light, daylight, is made up of all the different colours of the rainbow mixed together so that the light seems white, or see-through invisible. But whenever light lands on anything that can separate out its colours, that's when you actually get to see the colour of that thing. When light hits a tomato, the tomato's skin can absorb all the colours of light's spectrum, except red, which it reflects back away from it and into our eyes where we see it as red. Colour isn't fixed you see. Go get your crayons and I'll show you. We'll take the blue and the yellow and we'll use it to make green." Welcome my son, to the world of illusion and deceit. Where nothing is as it really seems. And not only within the visible wavelengths of light.

Tec, 9

There would be two murders. Unless one beat the other to the punch. Or the trigger. Or the carving knife. Or the ornamental table lamp with a loose wire that meant it flickered while it was on and made it impossible to read by. Like when you were reading on a train and it plunged into a tunnel. The only suspense being when you would re-emerge and get reading again, even though your eye had lost its place on the page. Not that either of his parents read books. Bradley was the only reader in the family. That lamp was the bane of his life, so there would be a certain sweet justice if it was smashed to smithereens. Not that he was advocating the commission of a crime. Just, well it was inevitable. Bradley's parents were at each other's throats and in all likelihood, that would no longer remain a mere figure of speech.

What could he do about it though? No felony had been committed at present. Detectives were always summoned after the event. To reconstruct how it had gone down from the trail of clues and evidence. The story of the deceased unfolded for them by these skilled, if brusque narrators. Law enforcers who could solely enforce the law once it had been broken. First aiders only applying the sticking plaster once the blood has already gushed so heavily that there was nothing left to staunch. So maybe it fell to him to proactively, well, act. Crime prevention. They already had a neighbourhood watch sticker in the bay window, didn't they? His parents could make the community safer and reduce crime just by easing back on one another.

Yet could Bradley be fully sure? One hundred and ten percent certain? He of such tender years, how could he imagine he knew everything about how the world worked? That, for all his prodigious reading, he had absorbed everything there was to know about the ways of adults? They were just stories after all. Avowedly fiction. Tales of dead bodies who one didn't feel all that bad about. Since they were the mere vessels for launching the task force of interesting stuff that was to follow. Patently he couldn't take the same view here and now. Not when the body was going to be one or other of his parents. The imminent blood on this particular carpet mattered. It would hurt. It was blood he himself was knitted from. Yet for all that novels were figments and fit-ups, he badly needed to bring about the state of affairs achieved by the end of any book. Whereby the detective had squared the circle and reset the world, so that all was right with society once again. An inescapably estimable outcome, but one Bradley would like to navigate towards without any corpus delicti. Going clean out of genre. To take all the mystery out of this situation, by forestalling murder altogether. That conundrum was what really needed solving.

Maybe this was just his parents at play. Locking horns like rutting stags. Although he wasn't quite sure what that said about his mother. But for all he knew, this was how they had always related to one another from the day they had met. Long before Bradley's entry into the world and his conscripted surveillance of them. He had seen youths in the street gesture cut throats and all lewd points south of there with twisted faces and snarling mouths towards one another, which had made him shrivel his body as small as possible. Only for them to approach each other and heartily clap them on the back with a big bear hug of an embrace. Perhaps his parents were replicating a slightly less energetic version of it as befits older people? His litany of literary detectives to date, had nothing to say on the matter. No illumination on this shadow play violence. He would have to go with his own instincts. A good detective had to be possessed of well-developed intuition after all. Was he getting an early induction with this case presented to him so precociously? There must have been cases that turned out not to be cases at all. Just nobody would write those in a novel, since they would be extremely dull to read.

So, what were his senses telling him? Was this going to end up with a pair of secateurs driven between the shoulder blades of his father? The black widow with her white floral print sundress and straw hat doing some brutal deadheading? Or rather with his mother's face crushed between the heated panels of the Corby Trouser press? The very instrument his dapper old man had been made to purchase for himself out of his own pocket. Why, because his wife refused to iron his pants (sorry, trousers, he mustn't slip into American), or because he didn't like the creases she wrought in them when she did oblige? They call it 'dressed to kill' after all, don't they? Oh god… This was all too easy to put together. Open and shut. There were only two suspects. Even in the best novels, you know the killer is somewhere in the story, having been shown to you by the author. The stories don't work if the killer turns out to be someone who has never put in an appearance until they are exposed as the slayer. His father was too miserly to call in for outside assistance to carry out the deed, solely in order to provide himself an alibi. His mother almost certainly, if she was going go so far as to commit the grievous act, would monopolise the pleasure for herself rather than share it out with an accomplice. Beyond a shadow of a doubt, there were only two in the frame, which would be reduced to the singular by the crime. One would remain with their shadow following them, while the other's would be expunged. But then he himself would be dogging the guilty party, a second shadow for them to contend with. His shadow would take up the cudgel and represent the fallen parent. No, no, no! It's already too late by then. It was tasked to him to preserve the light of both.

Means, motive, opportunity. That was the detective's holy trinity. Or was it an unholy trinity? More like a mantra perhaps, not even a Christian standard at all. Did they have good versus evil in Buddhism? He ought to investigate whether there were any Buddhist detective novels. Anyway, the means were already well established with a veritable arsenal of sharp edges and blunt objects camouflaged behind the everyday. Bradley knew that the family home had been made child-safe when he was a toddler. Seems like however it had never been rendered adult-safe. His parents had finally tied the knot when he was already four years old. He was a pageboy at their wedding. Sadly the role turned out to have nothing to do with books despite the promise in its name. He remembered trailing after them around the department store while they compiled their wedding gift list. Only now did he realise they were probably eyeing up objects and items of décor with a view to future lethality. Does that make the guest who bought the future murder weapon an accessory before the fact? Friend of the bride or groom? Maybe there were other persons of interest for him to quiz after all. He would have to bear it in mind.

The opportunity? Well they didn't have friends visiting very often that might stumble into the middle of a murder, so that wasn't any deterrent. Actually, that in itself could be an indication of what he was trying to wrestle with here. Maybe their friends were all put off by the constant quarrelling between his parents, never to lighten across their door again. Not an option for him, imprisoned on the other side of the slammer (and boy how much more did that door slam shut these days?) And what of the chances of a stranger bungling in? Cold callers did their business by phone these days and the vast majority of those were all automated machines. Singsong robotic voices rather than menacing heavy breathing. And he was beginning to suspect the whole neighbourhood watch thing was a bluff. Otherwise why was he the only one on the case here? Surely the neighbours next door could hear the yelled rows and draw precisely the same conclusion as he himself had done?

The only question therefore, was whether whichever parent made the first move, would they have the courtesy to wait for Bradley to be away from the house before the bloodletting? Hey, maybe that was his solution readily at hand? He could adopt a strategy of staying at home all the time just to let them know they were under constant scrutiny and thus deny them a clear run at their spouse. It would mean he'd have to drop out of school, but that was okay, more time reading books he actually wanted to read. Let's develop this thread to see if it holds water without going all soggy. His mum knew from his inoculations that the sight of blood made him blanch, if not to go the whole queasy hog and faint clean away to the floor. She would not inflict that on him. Unless… she planned to pin it on him. So having him unconscious there slap bang in the middle of the crime scene would play right into her hands. Each time he revived, he would see himself covered in blood and pass out again. Therefore time would not be a factor, since that afforded her a huge window to frame him with unimpeachably incriminating evidence, clean herself up and do whatever else she needed to establish her 'innocence'. Fiendish! Whereas his father was less aware of the debilitating effect of the sight of blood upon Bradley. But now he came to think about it, he remembered that film they had seen together, just the two of them and when the dog died in the movie, his father had started tittering while he himself was sniffling. His dad had told him to 'Man up', that life would hurl all sorts of terrible things for him to handle and deal with and that he would have to learn to cope. The sooner the better. So his dad might even expressly wait until he had come home in order to do the dread deed in front of him, as part of his initiation into the school of hard knocks. (Which begged the question why it had not already happened in order to accelerate Bradley's own development?) But then somehow his father would have to find a method to ensure Bradley's eternal silence. Gulp. Hopefully that meant more of a threat to hunt down and kill any future pets if he blabbed, rather than kill him here and now and double up on the body count. So no, opportunity was not really an issue for either of his merciless folks.

Indubitably therefore that returned him to motivation. And the same problem of how to judge the intent behind his parents' verbal viciousness. It was true that there was no history of any physical violence. And nor had either ever raised a hand in anger to him, but then they'd never ratcheted up their pronouncements towards him to the same febrile level they reserved for those directed at one other. Therefore, there was no exhibit A, B or C. No rap sheet. No file on either of them. God what had he been doing all these years, neglecting to keep proper records on the pair? What kind of detective would he make? Time for him to become hard-boiled rather than soft. Rather than scrambled. Perhaps this is what his father had been tempering him toward. That he had an inkling that he was going to get killed by his wife and was shaping Bradley to speak for his ghost.

Think, think, think! Even further back to the basics. Detective novels begin with an ending. For that of the life of the corpse. And their actual proper endings, are really far more significant than in other types of novels, because the identity of the murderer is revealed, as is the precise series of events as to how the act was committed. All tied up neatly with a bow. There is no room for ambiguity in detective novels, because someone must be brought to account for their villainy. However, the unfolding narrative of his own family had yet to really get underway. There was as yet no beginning signalled by a heinous act. Nevertheless, now Bradley found they already appeared to be at the ending, the sentencing phase. For his parents had sat him down on the couch under the spotlight of the flickering lamp. Some terrible interrogation this augured, since they presented a rare united front. Albeit both were twitching and fidgeting nervously, nay suspiciously he might have said. He idly wondered which was to play good cop and which bad, before remembering that he himself hadn't actually transgressed and executed anything meriting such hostile cross-examination. Had he? Yet if he was under suspicion, then he himself could hardly represent the investigating detective in this story. No wait, it happened all the time in novels. He would be suspended on full pay, so hopefully still receiving his pocket money. He would necessarily be forced to hand over his badge and gun, even though he didn't possess either in reality. Notions of beginnings and ends were dissolving. Even if nothing had actually come to an end, it seemed that he could be embarking on a new beginning in his life. Or maybe this was a warning, an affirmation he was destined for more of the same perhaps, though this circumstance seemed noticeably different. The jury was still out. Still, at least no one had died. Therefore he could only have doubts, that his role as a tec had in fact been called for at all.

His parents proceeded to present the facts. They were getting a divorce. Their words tripped over each other's as each begged his forgiveness and exonerated him from any guilt in the matter. So it was his body that the wrong-doing was being played over. Both seemed chock-full of remorse, but then again both seemed a little on the cagey side about who he was going to live with, once they sold the family home and moved to smaller domiciles. Bradley wondered who would get custody of the lamp.

Truth Fairy

It all started innocently enough. Conventionally too. A contract of exchange. A commercial piece rate. In return for the oblation of his offcast milk tooth, a coin of the realm would be deposited under Calvin's pillow while he slept. Money for old rope. Or pulp and enamel as in this case. Such is Calvin's budding skeptical nature, one speculates whether he bites down on the metal to test its authenticity, given the seeming disparity between the two sides of the swap. There are a lot of home-made counterfeit coins in circulation these days after all. But to chomp down on the bitter metal risks the detaching of further milky whites. Telescoping the whole process to a point where a currency note might be more apropos than coinage shrapnel. At least to Calvin's tender mind.

His mother is stymied as to how this covenant arose. For she well remembers the coin she received (of smaller denomination but larger diameter) as a child and her mother telling her of an even yet smaller value but larger disc of dull metal she herself had been bountied on the surrendering of a pearly white. Why reward a natural developmental staging post? As if one's baby gnashers could do aught else in the face of the pressure of their bigger and more incisive successors lying in wait just below the surface of the gums. If anything, parents should all be paying out to Evolution itself rather than its byproducts. Fine for humans to mark this rite of passage the first time it occurs, but to repeatedly shell out for an honorarium each time just seems redundant. As redundant as the shed premolars themselves.

Perhaps not. Maybe she is to seize the occasion to get across an important message, reinforced on each subsequent exigency, as she spins him the lie that only properly brushed teeth will yield healthy replacement teeth. And especially without the shedding of blood from gums improperly purged of redoubt food morsels and cranny cavities. That fiscal guerdon, is made out to be wholly contingent on good dental hygiene. A copper-bottomed incentive. She'd say a sweetener, but it's probably not a good word to bandy around the subject of dentition. Same way as she didn't offer up chocolate coins in place of the real thing. If compulsive Calvin had bitten down to test the integrity of those, he would have ended up ingesting the gold foil and invite choking.

Yet that's not the only canard parents serve up. Their side of the trade also had to appear disguised through a third-party agency. A shell company, or in this case a magical being. For rather than a transaction, this had to manifest as a substitution. For the tooth to disappear in order to reveal the specie in its place. Like alchemy. Only the adults were charged with taking measures to dispose of the tooth, in such a manner, that he could not discover its continued existence (the receptive pouch in his Baby

Book was full up with sample teeth, almost a veritable mouthful in its own right). Flushing down the toilet was no guarantee of oblivion. So it was kept in a handkerchief until the night before bin collection day, (since Calvin was not above scrambling through the house bins in search of reclaiming something adjudged to have been jettisoned precipitantly), whereupon it was finally launched into unsalvageable landfill dissolution.

For Calvin's part, the coin disappeared posthaste into the belly of his piggy bank, through the slotted gash in its loin. And thus was the Tooth Fairy invoked as the courier to expedite the compact, without commission, which was decent of her. Especially since she was potentially perjuring herself should it end up in litigation. Which it inevitably would when the duplicity could no longer be sustained. Father Christmas nearly got rumbled as plain old dad without any dedicated day of the year to his name last December. Stockings on the end of the bed soon to become elided in the anxious imagination, with stockings over the face of the masked intruder in Calvin's bedroom. The baby book enamel collection was explained as a museum loan. Their family Tooth Fairy benefactor seemed to alternate in gender, its hermaphroditic tendencies becoming expressed as one sex or the other according to which of them had a pound coin to hand.

And indeed this was inexorably how it played out. It's not just teeth that develop over time and maturation. So does the brain in its acuity. Calvin attained a stage where he continually reported that no coin had been received by morning's advent, even though his tooth had dematerialised in the night. She swore blind that the tooth fairy had visited if it had been her on point during the night. Her husband the same if it had been him. But then Calvin knew how to play his parents. The workaday fault lines and fissures in their relationship. Her husband would look dubiously on her claim, as if to challenge the veracity of her recollection. Equally she would look askance on his own powers of memory and habitual parsimony. How could either of them know for sure, since the Tooth Fairy went about her work sub-rosa? They went through the charade of turning the bedroom upside down in fruitless search. The case came off the pillow. The sheet stripped from the bed. The headboard pulled away from the wall. Yet the coin was nowhere to be found. And so she coughed up again. Paid double over the odds. Calvin fair minted it in the teeth of their moulded incredulity. The only child paid out on not twenty, but thirty-two deciduous fangs, the same number as a full adult set. Truly he had vaulted himself into adulthood in this sphere at least.

But there came a ceiling where she became fed up with her son's shell game. No more of this milk teeth milking her as milch cow. She had made a point of only having a single one pound coin in her purse, so that when the next tooth took its swan dive from his mouth, she raced to get to Calvin's pillow with coin in fist ahead of her husband. So now she definitively knew her purse was bereft. She further checked in the morning and still it yawned empty. Whereas Calvin spread his mouth open wide to aver that yet again the Tooth Fairy had been negligent in her duties. She had not indulged in fair exchange. Now his mother put her plan into action. First, she went to the bank and obtained some shiny, newly minted coins in exchange for a note. Once back home she took a kitchen knife to one of them, scoring and gouging and making little impression on the metal, but impression enough. She obliterated some of the serrations of the reeded edge, blurring and distorting just a few of these miniature Romanesque pillars so that they fell into one another. Through her close detailed work, she noticed for the first time that there were some tiny raised dots on the inside edge of the front wreathing HM Queenie's bust. With her new conversion to numismatics, she went to look them up online and found they were actually called 'denticles'. The symmetry of the name with the purpose of her doctored coin seemed to underwrite the logic of her scheme. This was not quite dye packs in with bank notes, but the aim was the same, to forestall and identify daylight robbery. The final plank of the plan entailed that she would have to break into Calvin's piggy bank, to observe the incriminating coin she currently held in her hand. But such a breach of trust seemed like a small price to pay in pursuit of the truth.

And sure enough, when she was able to conclusively buttonhole Calvin over his mendacity, the trespass involved in her subterfuge was hurled back at her in withering juvenile accusation. But she countered surehandedly that he had been stealing, embezzling and extorting the Tooth Fairy and worse, lying to his parents. Calvin grinned gap-toothed and simply and quietly riposted, that so had she and dad to him. He had known, since the last devaluation of the currency, that the Tooth Fairy didn't exist.

Gravamen

Petra was a hoarder. She never threw anything of her life away. He parents may have maintained a baby book of her burgeoning evolution, but her own collated omnibus was far more comprehensive than her parents' muster and it continued on into her present status as a teen. Baby books were pensioned off not long after the page recording 'first words'; as if somehow the cradle of language put an end to the individual ontogenesis of a baby, so that it was no longer worth recording. (When of course it was actually the other way round, that language and self-expression far more render character than physical appearance does). Nevertheless, Petra took up the slack from there. She kept her reading primers, and indeed they had become the locus for her own notes and observations of self. An omphalos marking her entry into the world of language, which she kept updated with more complex branches of thought, than that which emanated from building blocks of 'Tigers' and 'Worms' illustrating the alphabetic characters within. For her, these single letter, single illustrated words, functioned the same as monks' illuminated majuscules attesting to grace and exaltation.

And yet the older she got, the more Petra realised that animals were not so ennobled as their primary status in human instruction suggested. On the relevant page of her primers, (since the animals used to embody the alphabet could vary from book to book), Petra noted down each instance of both veneration and degradation of the animal depicted there as she came across them in her research. And to her horror, the latter soon far outweighed the former. On some pages the depravity heaped on the subject creature was such, that she was forced to write her notes over the cartoon depiction of the endangered animal itself, thus further underscoring the sense of erasure and threat. We present here Exhibits A, B and C, all the way through to Z, arranged in the order in which they were discovered.

T IS FOR TURTLE / TORTOISE

Myth – Personification (!) of creation and longevity. Bears the burden of the world on its back (literally in the case of the tortoise who has its entire world borne there). Flat earth and domed sky/heavens, symbolised by the architecture of its shell. The fable of the tortoise and the hare, more haste less speed. Tenacity. Playwright Aeschylus killed by a tortoise slipping from the grasp of a predator eagle and falling down from a great height straight on to his noggin. Reality or myth?

Reality – Turtle soup, ugh! Tortoise racing, oh ha-ha. Teenage Mutant Ninja Turtles. Charles Darwin's ship "The Beagle" bringing home Giant Galapagos Turtles which never made it to British soil, instead serving as slap-up meals for the crew. Needless to say, most species endangered through the usual; habitat predation, food/ medicine and pet trade. Mea culpa. Tortoise non-native to UK (too perishing cold). I- my family, had several, all culled by our failings in provision for their hibernation. They already have their homes, yet we put them in the secondary house of a wooden box. Their coffin. Stupidly we kept at it. Similar to trying to grow avocados from their stones, skewered by a four tooth-picked cruciform, but this is off topic. The beauty of the tortoise's shell, spoiled by the whitewash painting of its name, or house number, for identification purposes. Same as our recycling bins.

E IS FOR ELEPHANT

Myth – Hindu world elephants as the four cardinal points of the compass. Ganesh, apex divinity and symbolising wisdom. An elephant shaking itself dry held to cause earthquakes. The myth of the elephants' graveyard.

Reality – Poached for ivory. A beast of burden used to clear forests for logging, thus unwittingly participating in destroying its own habitat. YouTube videos of elephant football, balancing acts and pedalling cars, grotesque inverse of the flea circus. (Any circus animal act actually; see *Lions*; *Sea Lions*; *Horses*). The elephant in the room, how we humans exploit animals for our own entertainment.

Theory – primitive man had to mimic animals to be a successful hunter. Move like them, smell like them, make calls like them and have the same hides as them to get close enough to strike. This accounts for the origin of animal myths, as man accorded animals their true power and their role in supernatural attribution for these mystical processes. But when so called rationality, a "superior" appreciation of cause and effect and the advances of science began to erode supernatural explanations, man turned the tables and took revenge on his previous subordinate status by making animals ape us. And the whole damn web of relationships fell apart and we turned the ecosystem to shit. 'A' is for 'anthropomorphism'.

B IS FOR BEE

The only animal whose name wholly embodies the letter it represents. The nonsensical acoustic of 'B is for Bee', of course what else could it bee? Phoneme morphs into morpheme morphs into lexeme. Spelling bees, when the ear can't even distinguish between the letter and the word. Bzzzy as a bee. Buzz bee. Can go on like this for ever.

Myth – Bees have few negative associations in myth, presumably due to their providence with honey. They are held to endow human kind with eloquence, spread on our lips as honeyed talk, poetry, music (buzzing/humming) etc. They are also linked to prophecy and knowledge of the future, (including the weather), the Oracle at Delphi being known as the Delphic Bee and Apollo's gift of prophecy being bestowed upon him by a trinity of bee goddesses. They are also associated with wealth and good fortune, though in some contexts swarms of bees portend a bad omen.

Reality – For all the bee's knees, the species appears to be(e) making a beeline for death. Since the bees are all disappearing, and we haven't the first idea why. You better bee-leave it.

C IS FOR CROCODILE

As the creature is so fearsome, its depiction in alphabet and reading primers is softened to a considerable degree. To the same extent I have seen cuddly crocodile soft toys. Go online, you can see felt figures that make them look more like frogs, fish, moles, anything other than crocs. But then that's entirely consistent with the origins of its name, the Greek's original 'crocodilos' cast them as 'lizards'. Close, but no cigar.

Myth – Venerated in Ancient Egypt, the god Sobek and the Nile city dedicated to him called Crocodopolis. In the Guatemalan, *Popol Vuh* codex the crocodilian Zipacna (a cayman in fact), defeated the host of four hundred boys who had enlisted his help in erecting a hut before turning on him, by pulling down the building to crush them. Course he was fatally punished for just trying to defend himself. A law of Man not Nature. Don't think there exists a concept of 'revenge' in the animal kingdom.

Reality – Handbags, belts and shoes, gross. We shed crocodile tears for the victims of our fashion. The viral meme of the python whose body burst by trying to swallow an alligator. Presented as an allegory for not biting off more than you can chew. What we conveniently overlook is that the Burmese Python is not native to Florida, so that it was likely a pet abandoned when it began to grow beyond domestic confines.

F IS FOR FOX

The quick brown fox jumped over the lazy dog. The

totemic animal chosen to mark the transition from the privileged scribe, to the democratisation of writing signified by the mass-produced typewriter. And the computer and tablets nowadays have seen no need to change the ordering. The dog could have been a contender, but it was too indolent. The quick-witted fox made off with the spoils.

Myth – Oh my god, where to start with this one? Silver Fox a wise creator, through the Promethean fox character who brought mankind fire, all the way to tricksters and fraudsters. Shapeshifting demon soul-stealers. The causers of the Northern Lights. Subject of many fables and fairy tales. Gingerbread anyone?

Reality – Rabies control, yeah right. And next they came for the badgers... Pest control. Wait a minute, Australia only developed its particularly bad fox problem after originally introducing the non-indigenous animal to continue the old Pommy tradition of hunting with hounds (therefore colonised for a second time from Britain). Now they sterilise the foxes instead. Very sporting. Very Nazi. And of course fox-hunting itself, which the so-called animal-loving British public have at long last outlawed. But it's a clear manifestation of the city-country divide and pressure is building to reverse the ban, because apparently, us urbanites just don't understand the country ways. Funny, seeing as we have our own urban foxes here in town. I've seen them with my own eyes, beautiful creatures utterly unmoved by us humans, as they insouciantly trot along the pavement ambling into the drives of houses. A whole new modern mythology has grown up around the urban fox, how they attack pet cats and dogs and bite babies, fostered by scaremongering newspapers.

Actually, they're damned useful, as people are so unhygienic that we are overrun by rats – you're never more than ten feet away from a rat – and the foxes help trim their numbers for us. Now that's proper pest control. The fur industry, fox stoles, never was there a more fitting word… Oh my god, where to end with this one?

S IS FOR SHEEP

A difficult word to offer a child for encapsulating a letter in many ways, seeing that is both singular and plural. On the other hand, an obvious choice for the character, since it is the animal most likely to be witnessed outside of the cat basket and dog kennel by a toddler. Though it is almost inevitably going to be introduced and nominated by its onomatopoeia, 'Baa-Baa'.

Myth – I dunno. The fluffier the creature seems the less significance in myth. We tend not to elevate the commonplace we see out of our window, into the divine. Though saying that, cows are sacred in India and cats in Ancient Egypt so maybe the theory doesn't hold water. But there is not much for sheep. Wolves in sheep's clothing. The Golden Fleece. Odysseus escaping from Polyphemus' cave by clutching the underside of the cyclops' flock as he leads them out to pasture. Each with a theme of duplicity and disguise. The 'black sheep'. Themes of shepherding and flocks, lending themselves perfectly to organised religions with a priest class to lead them. The purity and innocence of lambs. The ram sacrificed in place of Isaac. Jesus as Lamb of God sacrificed for our sins. The Paschal Lamb as Egyptian first born were victims of the Angel of Death, but Jewish firstborns spared, the mark of sheep's blood on their lintels as the Exterminating Angel passes over. The supposed mark of civilisation, with dumb animals in place of human sacrifice. Not in my book. That is no progress from barbarism at all.

Reality – Seeing that sheep are so central to human diet and raiment, surely there is no way on earth we are going to screw this species up? Other than feeding them ground up remains of their relatives infected with scrapie and this contaminating the animal feed for cows, so prompting Mad Cow Disease (see also *Cow*). That's what you get for turning ruminants into carnivores.

W IS FOR WHALE

Myth – The sinker of ships and the devourer of sailors. Its sheer scale made it ripe for mythologising and legend. The Biblical Leviathan. Jonah's enlightened deliverance. Stories aplenty of sleeping whales mistaken for islands, for man to land and start cooking their food when the fire wakes up the beast and it dives, taking all down into Davy Jones' locker.

Reality – Whaling. A moratorium, note not a ban, but a 'moratorium'. The etymological roots of this word mean 'a delay'. Iceland, Norway, Japan, just whetting their harpoons in interim. An orca kills its trainer in the freak show that is a marine theme park and people are shocked and surprised. Do you know how cruel that particular captivity is? Swapping the limitless ocean for a cramped aquarium? The rash of whales beaching themselves and inevitably expiring out of the water, particularly along our UK coastline. Though causes unknown at present, increased human sea traffic impedes whale song communication and likely fouls up their navigation.

V IS FOR VULTURE

(not a creature you find in any toddler's reading primer, but an appendix supplied by me, with a picture printed off from the internet and glued on over the pre-existing 'V is for Violin' or 'V is for Van.' Or the abstract 'V is for Vegetables', where 'V' is apparently for carrot, cucumber and cauliflower. 'V' is for pepper too, both the one that comes in lots of colours and the one you get in a shaker next to the salt. Tomato sauce that comes out of plastic tomato squeezers, even though tomatoes are a fruit not a vegetable... The whole conceit collapses in on itself. In some early American abecedaries, the letter 'V' along with 'I' is missed out altogether. Too hard to twin with a morally fortifying image presumably.)

Myth – Darkness and disease. Bad omens. Tricksters. Power/totem animal. In several mythologies it is the spread of a giant vulture's wings that eclipses the sun. Also in some traditions, represents the eternal unseparated union of light and dark, day and night (primordial, inchoate state? Further work required). Associated with dirt and the unclean, when in fact it represents the complete opposite, as a purifier, or hoover-upper if you will. Dead carrion rife with germs only the vulture is immune to and removes them from the potential human bagging area. Hercules slew the vulture that was tearing out Prometheus' liver. Harpies were female heads and bodies, with a vulture's claws and wings, gee thanks. In Egyptian mythos the ultimate symbol of motherhood because of how protective towards their young they are. Sacred symbol of Isis. At the top of the heap in the hieroglyphic alphabet, representing the letter 'A'. Romulus and Remus arguing over exact location of Rome, settled their dispute by watching a flight of vultures. They must have apprehended their future empire would be born in blood. The word 'augury' comes from tracing the flights of birds for omens.

Reality – Despite their bad rep and association with dirt, man does not really go after vultures, probably out of superstitious fear. Some cultures also recognise the vital environmental role played by these scavengers and foster this through 'sky burials', where a lack of deep soil in mountainous regions precludes human burial, so the flesh is offered to the birds for removal. Yet even this undertaking function, now threatens to wreak a customary human forfeit. Since the chemicals pumped into our herds (see *Cows*) are toxic to the vultures, so feeding on any accidental carcasses has led to an unintentional cull of the birds, like the Pharaohs killing their pyramid builders and consigning them to the very same tombs they designed. Human manufactured chemicals wreak havoc on the toughest of digestive and immune systems, that otherwise cope with any bacteria thrown at them by Nature.

D IS FOR DONKEY

Myth – Workhorse, stubborn, stupid, servile and a joker. Symbol of Ra. Jesus rides into Jerusalem on a donkey. The bray of a donkey alerts the faithful that the devil is near and that they are to turn towards Allah. King Midas has his ears turned into those of an ass, Bottom in *Midsummer Night's Dream* suffers the whole hog for his entire head.

Though Shakespeare is not myth, it is fiction. Even if it draws on myth for its setting. Myth can be literature, but is literature necessarily myth? "Iliad", Norse Sagas, "Popol Vuh" are both, but at what point does that cease? When does myth just become prosaic fiction? (More study needed).

Reality – The beast of overburden. TV documentaries lifting the lid on the cruel treatment of donkeys. Donkey sanctuaries. More charities than you can shake a stick at dedicated to ameliorate the same. And yet in the US they have donkey basketball matches as a fundraising event. Go figure. I am not without blame on this front. As a kid I went on donkey rides at the beach. Ignorance is no defence. Children have no mitigation. Their parents fail them when they do not instruct them in any and all this abuse. These books, these ridiculously idealised books, are utterly misleading in what they portray. 'E is for elephant' should have a picture of a bloodied tuskless carcass. 'F is for fox' should be represented by the bloodied spume of a fox caught by hounds; with the hunters holding aloft head, tail and paws as their trophy and the dogs tearing into what's left. Sure it's upsetting, but children need to see the unflinching reality. Otherwise they will never grow up into adults who seek to bring about change. Actually, these books are worse than misleading, they're pernicious. How can they create such affection in us through these innocent images and yet be yoked to the letters of an alphabet that represents man's lethal superiority over fauna?

In a rage Petra gathered up all these primers and infant books she had so lovingly preserved and took them out into the garden. She threw them down in a heap, ripped out pages to serve as firelighters and ignited them to create her very own Saüberung on the lawn. Unfortunately she wasn't aware that the books had landed over a depression in the grass (probably caused by a burrowing animal) and that a hedgehog had taken up temporary residence there for a nap. Woken only once the fire had taken hold, the creature kicked away at the press of paper leaves, thus spreading some of the pages which are the ones saved here to form the incomplete record of Petra's ruminations. Unfortunately, the hedgehog is not as a mythic whale woken by fire, so the sheer mass of the books prevented the hedgehog from being able to successfully escape and it died bellowing its tiny screams which Petra could not hear beyond the crackle of the pulp. This partial record is introduced as evidence in the prosecution of Petra for cruelty to animals, in the form of the malicious burning of a live animal to death.

Laud of Misrule

Pets are said to resemble their masters. Well this punchman's transformation into Mr Punch was almost complete. Being perennially crouched over in his booth had curved him like his hunchback taskmaster. The salt in the seaside air had corroded the elasticity of his ligaments, so that he was now little more supple than his wooden paymaster. The palsy in his face had drooped his nose towards his chin, to resemble the physiognomy of his lord and master. His emphysema entailed that through his vaporous lungs, he now spoke just like the swazzled whoremaster. (Whenever there was any dialogue in his dreams at night, the words were delivered through a swazzle, that's how much his lifelong occupation had seeped into him).

Only his hands were ever above the parapet and they were sheathed inside the wooden prophylactic that were his puppets. His deformities ducked down and shrouded in the witness protection behind the skein of his booth. He was invisible despite the naked pleasure and entertainment he was actively bringing to the little ones just beyond the flimsy tenting. His gift to them, a rare, precious commodity in these days of satiety and prematurely jaded palates. There was something exotically archaic about Punch and Judy that still unfailingly provoked ecstatic delight in its audiences. Although even kiddie curiosity had seemingly become dulled, as no longer did any tearaways furtively sneak up and try and pull back the booth's canvas to reveal him working away inside. He was anonymous to the grown-ups and uninteresting to the kids. Irrelevant to both. The magic didn't just happen by itself damn it.

The decibel level of the shrieks beyond the booth had increased. He surmised that more punters had stopped by for a gander. Didn't matter that they had missed half the show. Its episodic structure meant anyone could dip in and out of it and still derive an understanding. Perfectly distilled for today's short attention spans. Or non-attention spans, seeing as he could picture all the parents there sat gawping at their phones. 'That's the way to do it,' as Mr Punch cued up the chorus for their offspring in a familiar refrain, even as their parents refrained from doing anything that could be construed as interacting with him, or their own kids. He couldn't help himself from repeating Mr Punch's self-satisfied apothegm, as an ironic counterpoint to the parents' self-absorbed failings. Complete waste of time him coming up with lines that offered the parents a guffaw or two, without the kids quite appreciating what was being said, although with the acceleration of childhood these days who knew? 'That's the way to do it'. And again. The pitch of the kids' response grew higher as they rebutted Punch's immoralism with a hearty 'Oh no it isn't!' Almost as if they were trying to wrest their parents' attention back for themselves. He had them eating out of the puppet-bedecked palm of his hands. It was like he was a Pied Piper, only his instrument was the swazzle and he could march them wherever he chose, even right off the beach into the sea and perish the little perishers. He caught himself, judging that Punch's catchphrase catechism was running out of legs. No stamina, that was the problem, sat on their backsides all day in front of TV and computer screens. He smoothly elided back into the story, as Mr Punch tossed the felled cadaver of Judy off stage to prepare for the next contender. If a puppet hewn from a tree falls among a forest of blunted sensibilities, can anyone hear her scream?

How the politically correct mob had castrated him. No more was Punch allowed to thwack his baby with a stick (and no hangman ending up in his own noose either). Although by way of compensation it had given rise to the gag that prompted the loudest laugh, in the form of Mr Punch sitting on the baby when charged by Judy with the onerous task of 'babysitting'. Which was after all, what he himself was doing for the duration of any kid sat there on the sand, or in the lap of their absented parent. What a joke these present-day Puritans were, presiding over the greatest collapse of morality ever witnessed, fiddling while Britain burned through a tsunami of parental neglect. How could the politicians and social nannyers dare say Punch and Judy incited domestic abuse, even as these kids spilled gallons (sorry, litres) of blood on their murderous computer games? No one ever said a kid went out and assaulted someone because of a Punch and Judy show now did they? Even during that so-called happy slapping phase, it wasn't with any slapstick in hand now was it? Mr Punch's body count, which the kids chimed out the numbers in unison towards the apotheosis of the show, was nothing on the mounds of corpses piled up in those horrendous video games. They even have them in the arcades on the pier now. In a last desperate attempt to create a home from home to appeal to these restive, sneering ingénues. The world is their oyster with everything that's available to them, yet these costive kids persist with the shrunken horizons of holing up in their bedrooms. And believe him, he knew from costive, what with that and his piles. Something he didn't mirror from Mr Punch.

He was forever surprised that in such a world of chaos as they resided in presently, that Punch's anarchic rule-flouting still even registered. That the forces of law and order, in the shape of the policeman, showed up at all for a report of Punch's domestic violence, was a deviation from the reality of his audience's experience. And Punch's outrageous behaviour would hardly be regarded as outré in this day and age. In his origins, Punch represented the exception from the rule, the citizen of Albion who didn't abide by laws and decency. But he couldn't explain the appeal now, when there was nothing left to subvert and everyone functioned as their own lord and lady of misrule. Perhaps it's because Punch just bloody always wins and the grockles can aspire to that forlorn dream. After all, these poor lambs are the ones who have to holiday here rather than jet off to Disneyland. They were truly the benighted and the dispossessed. For these seasiders of last resort, this beach-combed jetsam, Punch is top dog. Chief thug. Head of the postcode gang that no one can knock off his perch and supplant, for all comers always get beaten down by him. The punchman's fevered imagination was beginning to run away with him. He might say he had a touch of sunstroke, only squatting down behind the booth's awning, he never got to feel the sun on the crown of his head.

The kids had regathered themselves and were shouting warnings to Mr Punch about the crocodile behind him aiming to gobble up Punch's sausages. Like the flipping pantomime barker up there on the pier trying to snaffle his punters away from him. Which to judge by the desultory queues he saw when he was packing up after each day's final performance, was in more trouble to retain an audience than his own humble little sideshow. (He shouldn't snipe, both Punch and Panto were the bastard progeny of Commedia Dell'Arte). These days the menace and threat was not just lurking behind, but all around you and no one ever saw it coming. But that's progress for you. And once something is lost, it's extinct and there's no getting it back. When the politically correct mob decree that sausages do not form part of a healthy diet within our land of ten ton parents and their obese spawn, sat out there yonder bevelling into the sand and instead order him to puppeteer strings of falafel balls, the comedic effect would be purged forever. The timeless narrative shifted into the modern day and defanged. Mind you it made sense that he removed the Devil, Punch's traditional final foe, from the litany of finger wagging aimed at his humble show. Since though clownish, it is Punch himself who is positively diabolical. What need of any supernatural agency to hang evil upon, when at last perhaps folk need to acknowledge that malignancy lurks within themselves? Only those nitwits who simplify everything, so as to deem puppeted baby beating, or medical doctors who administer cures with a slapstick treatment of their own, as politically incorrect, could fail to appreciate that human beings are morally ambiguous. Fully capable of both the most delightful and the most wretched of behaviours. That he could both love his audience and simultaneously desire to walk them all off the pier for a mass drowning of the little darlings. But the immemorial Devil was an utterly duplicitous device. If the Devil bested Punch, then this was Punch being punished for his heinous behaviour. If Punch overcame the Devil, then this demonstrated the possibility of even the basest of mortals being able to resist and defeat the embodiment of vice. Nice double bind that.

Punch and Judy took their bows. The children didn't seem to know that this signalled the end and serve for a prompt to their appreciation. Why would they? None of them would have been to a theatre in their life. Chances are there were no circuses left for them to visit either, thanks to the animal rights mob. And their parents were still too glued to their phones to notice and guide them. No, his artform and its story lines had remained essentially unchanged in half a millennium. It was the audience which had changed irrevocably.

Father Trismus

Open wide like a good girl.

Even at that tender age it felt like a violation. Less intimate than a subsequent pap smear, yet more invasive somehow.

Aw come on Cassie, nice and wide now.

Again, somehow, I had an understanding of what was involved. We both did. An unverbalised negotiation. You, jabbing the plastic spoon in the vicinity of my kisser; me, bobbing and weaving in my highchair to duck your thrusts. My hands thrown up against my mouth like a boxer covering up, although there were never any real blows to parry of course. Our prandial bout of sparring. Yet we both knew. I may have launched my hands up as barrage balloon resistance, nevertheless I would be sucker punched each time. On the ropes, strapped into my chair by restraints. Counted out. There was always a proportion of the victuals you would insist on me consuming, a marker of sufficient nourishment in your eyes. Perhaps designated by the exposure of the floor of the plastic dish from its alimentary gloopy glaze. A glacially slow revelation of what lay beneath the mush. Once we had attained that inverse summit, I could be excused further repast. On the other hand, my display of non-co-operation masked my ulterior stratagem. Of part-spoon servings artfully diverted on to the blotter of my bib. Or dollops displaced stealthily on to the tray of my high chair, anywhere but the intended destination of my gob. Mummer me improvising caked greasepaint, by resorting to daubing the unctuous food pigments I was being proffered. Mother you, inspecting the cuisine debris scattered all around the feeding zone. An acceptable spoilage rate. Comestible casualties for the cause. Cannon fodder contingency.

Clear your plate. There are children who are starving in Africa who would leap at the chance to have what you're proposing to let go to waste there.

I tried to call her bluff once. I got up from the table in the middle of (their measurement) / having finished (my gauge) the meal. Challenged as to where I thought I was going, when in fact I knew precisely. I said I would return imminently, which I did, having gone to the bureau in the lounge, opened its credenza thing which housed the Russian doll-like Rolodex of all their friends' contact details and brought it back into the kitchen, together with a thick cream envelope. I sat back down and started to scoop the mess of pabulum from my plate into the chartaceous pouch with my fingers. It was oozing back out, momentarily returning me to the sensations of my high chair days, before I finished my task and looked up expectantly at their stunned faces. Holding my food-coated hand ostentatiously away from the Rolodex, as if I were awaiting the pulp to dry like nail varnish, I gingerly started flipping the index cards round with the digits of my non-besmirched hand. I pointedly progressed one revolution through the entire set of cards, still without comment from either parent, although my father had balled one fist into the palm of the other hand and propped the conjoined pair under his chin as if to buttress his scrutiny. "Well, I don't see an address of anyone in Africa here. So who should I send it to exactly?" Of course the rug was completely pulled from under me when just a year or so later, so many of my favourite pop stars were performing on stages around the world raising money to beat the famine in Ethiopia. Images of children with stomachs distended by malnutrition, patently unable to leap at anything at all. Still, my mother never resorted again to that particular appeal to my conscience.

Broom broom. The car wants to come into the garage Cassie.
Open wide. Beep beep! Let the car in…
Broom broom broom."

Our garage was overrun by rats. There's no way on earth I would readily be so accommodating as to open either the back door to gain ingress, or the electronic open sesame for cars to coast in. Even though once I turned seventeen, passed my driving test first time of asking, and had gone and bought my own runaround, still I never parked it inside. That garage is a place of nightmares. In the small hours I could hear them scurrying on its flat roof which lay adjacent to my bedroom wall. Even in my lowest teenage moments, that period of revved up consideration of putting an end to this miserable existence of mine, the garage though it supported the sturdiest ceiling beam of the residence, would never play host to suspending a noose. I could neither bring myself even to enter the demesne of the rodents, let alone offer lifeless carrion me up for a murine meal. And since my oral anxieties closed off any option of overdosing on medicine cabinet remedies, my nascent suicide drive quickly ran out of viable solutions. My parents called in pest control to liberate and restore the garage into human hands, but the rats were back by the next spring. The exterminator shrugged his shoulders and proclaimed we possessed the perfect conditions that rats favoured. He indicated the path of their rat run, which consequently closed off the garden to me as well.

Put the petrol pump in the car. Fill it up with fuel to drive.

And drop a lit match on the forecourt around the pumps and let's be done with this whole sorry farrago.

Neeeyaagh! The airplane needs to land on the runway.
Permission to land Cassie?

So I'm the flight controller in the watchtower, am I? Well there is a smoke contrail rising from the spoon's cargo, but I think we'll let the battered old kite circle a bit more yet. I suppose I'll have to let it land eventually though. Don't want all those pulverised blood and guts on my conscience. Is my tongue supposed to serve for a runway? Pocked full of cracks and craters as it is? Better divert to another airstrip. Actually, this was all a tad presumptuous, since at the time I had yet to enter the fuselage of a plane (excluding the memory blank of my first eighteen months of existence and any womb-borne journeys I may have unknowingly undertaken). And yet here I was, expected to know exactly what the processes of landing a plane involved, further taxiing on the runway, then disembarking the passengers down a long steel dribble of steps while losing some of the baggage spit out on to the carousel, next to have suspicious looking folk strip-searched in Customs or Passport control… Hey wait a minute, why didn't I erect my own Passport control and Customs at the border of my lips? Prevent any alien fare passing into my mouth and we would have avoided all these diplomatic incidents. Time to pilot my own heap. Permission to take off Cassie?

Toot toot! The train wants to enter the tunnel.

And we all know what Freud said about trains and tunnels now don't we? Maybe this is why I refuse to go down on a man. Actually it's only likely to be one of a few reasons. There seems to be a persistent theme of transport and propellants. But that's okay, that's how I regard food by and large anyway. It holds few if any delights for me. Merely sustenance to continue functioning, now that I have come to the meagre conclusion I may as well persevere with life for its slim pickings on offer. Probably why I can only be bothered enough to eat pre-cooked meals that I can just shove in the microwave. Minimises the washing up too. Double bubble and squeak.

How do you know you don't like it if you haven't even tried it?

Now we had reached the stage where rather than tall tales supposed to hoodwink me, instead there were direct, plaintive, exasperated pleas. But even passing over the fact you no longer troubled to disguise your intentions, I'm led to believe that visual presentation of food forms an important component of how our senses structure taste. And your burnt offerings dear mama, more often than not, just didn't cut the mustard. My vanguard sight taste buds passed the message on down the line. Avoid at all costs.

You need to eat up all your greens to grow big and strong.

Cauliflower is not green. Even when you cook it in the same pan as the broccoli, so its colour leaches into the cauliflower and turns it a hideous shade of taupe. There's a metaphor in there somewhere for all of us, though dashed if I can unscramble it. And as for growing up big and strong, you mean like an Amazon, or a woman with pneumatic mammaries perhaps? As seems to be all the rage. Actually, my food issues have nothing to do with self-image and body dysmorphia. Rather they all centralise and coagulate around just one locus, my maw and the unseen part of it at that. Nothing that anyone else can stare into and pronounce upon. Not even a dentist is granted admission to the cavities within. So those ruses offering ice cream and other dessert treats as a reward for eating the less palatable meat, fish and savouries, didn't really distort the relative values of both food groups in my mind. I still credit I am even-handed in the amounts of each I consume. Being that I am equally indifferent to both.

And yet the most formative assault on my mouth was delivered without any word payload. There was a wholesale lack of pretence at magical narrative transmutations in order to get me to part my lips. Father was less patient and less whimsical than mother. Not for him the differential equation, of food to mouth meets means of conveyance and energy. First, he prodded the spoon at my resolutely closed lips. Then he manipulated the tip to prise my labia apart, whereupon the food's progress was halted by my front teeth being clamped together presenting a sheer enamel barricade (now they no longer perch flush on top one to the other). He assailed this obstacle by using the spoon as a battering ram, plunging hard against my teeth and making me relinquish their steadfastness more through shock than actual pain, though the nerve endings in my gums were aflame. Penetrating on deeper, my tongue fenced with the spoon, diverting it this way and that with its flicks, while managing also to present another impermeable vertical hindrance. He brutally knocked it aside with an overpowering thrust, which drove the spoon right into the membrane of one of my cheeks. That one did hurt and brought about my submission to tamely swallowing the pap.

It also planted the mental seed of me never liking food to touch the sides of my mouth, rather only to be siphoned straight down the gullet. And a lifetime of festering mouth ulcers in the violated vicinity. There is to be no kissing of any prince ushering in a happy ending. For I'd been the recipient of a powerful, prosaic story that day. One that did away with the fanciful, the bargaining, the fictive, in all its deceitful elements. And the one I'm still trying to escape from today. To change the galling ending.

Vade Mecum

He was so bored of reading this story aloud night after night after night. But his son Eric always insisted it had to be part of the prose lullaby recital. Though the world turned nightly, for his son it was as if the day was held frozen, until they had passed through the gateway of this one particular story to bring the shutter down on it. He had tried teasing Eric about not doing the story. In an attempt to forge a little shared verbal routine, a back and forth slapstick. A shared catechism where each played their prescribed role. But such had been the vehemence of his son's dissension, that he hastily backtracked and abandoned his immediate hope of any jocose father-son communion.

Often his attention drifted while he was reading it, until he was brusquely snapped back by the piqued reproach of his son. Eric it seemed, was a most demanding stickler for puerile convention. It was at such moments he could really feel for his wife, stuck at home all day and every day during daylight hours, solely with this infantile level of company.

One evening, horror of horrors, they couldn't locate the

book. They searched high and low. Momentarily he tried to recall if this had been a stratagem of his own, in an attempt to break the stranglehold. Or perhaps a fiendish ploy of his wife, lashing out at him through her own exasperated pique over some domestic infraction on his part. But he quickly dismissed both as unrealistic explanations. The early evening was his wife's sole bout of respite, so she was hardly going to imperil that by prompting a diplomatic incident. Actually scrub that, less of an incident, more an outbreak of cluster bombing to judge by his son's relentless detonations. They searched high and low, him trying to lessen the stakes by turning it into a pirate's treasure hunt game. It didn't work, Prolonged John Mither went about the quest as if on a search and destroy mission, as he turned his own room upside down.

His father ruefully thought the book had picked itself up and taken off for somewhere to quietly self-immolate. Freeing itself of this monstrous regime of abuse, both by his own rendition of its tale and the slave-driving overseeing of his scion. He pleaded with his son to forego the story just this one night. Eric steadfastly refused, stating that he wouldn't go to sleep until he'd heard it. Now there was a paltry challenge thought his father, since he'd read the flipping story so many times he probably knew it by heart. So he bade his son to lie back down and settle himself on his pillow. He would still have his story this bedtime.

There would be no straying of attention on his part tonight. It would be all about concentrating on every word, for Eric would pick him up on any slight deviation from the sacred text. However, it presented a different sort of agony as he was relaying the tale, since his mind was racing ahead to recall the next line. Thereby he was not injecting his customary inflection into the words that so brought the story alive for his son. There was none of the abiding swagger oozing from the voices of the characters. The animal noises were even more reedy and indistinguishable than usual. True to form, his son chided him for each flat intonation, every missed vocal flourish. "I'll tell you what, you know it so well, why don't you tell the story?" his father gauntleted. A retort he was overly familiar with, from the dynamic at play on those rare occasions when he and his wife were in company and she would take over the narrating of his anecdotes. Like his mother, Eric declined the offer. Orthodoxy must prevail.

They bumbled and bodged their way through the tale to the bitter, contested end, whereupon his father promised him they would never have a repeat of such an atrocity. He would go to the bookshop the following day and buy a new copy of the book. Tragically it turned out that the new version was in fact a new edition, with some minor changes in the text, which were of course immediately spotted and jumped upon by this most tyrannical of precocious editors. Gradually the book fell out of their established evening canon, but it entailed their shared emotional bond was never quite the same either. Even though he was utterly above blame, his father felt guilty at this turn of events. He went on the internet to see if he could find the same edition of the book, but to no avail.

However he struck lucky in another way. He realised that the book had been turned into a film and he tracked down a DVD of it. He wanted to make it special. When his son was having a bath, he snuck upstairs and wheeled the television in from his own sleeping quarters and turned his son's nursery into a screening room. He sat his bemused offspring down on the bean bag in front of the screen and began the show. Eric, perhaps inevitably, was not standing for such an abominable sacrilege and rose from his perch to remonstrate with his father. They had perhaps their first full exchange of views man-to (little) man and it could have gone in one of either two ways. He could have taken it as categorical evidence of his son starting to etch out his own individual view of the world and welcomed the incipient tread on the travelator of maturation. Instead he took it as evidence of his son's ineffable stubbornness to remain self-centred and infantile and decided then and there, to turn away from his seemingly insatiable solipsism and distance himself by increments. His mother could deal with his inundations from now on.

It was a pity that the father hadn't heard out his son's objections to his intended treat, itself designed as some sort of rite of passage into receiving different narrative forms. Since under his own auspices, Eric had actually constructed the rather unimpeachably sophisticated notion, that the film had presented him with an entirely alien version of the beloved story which they had created together over the many renditions. His father and his joint version had been laid down like a fine wine and fermented to perfection in Eric's imagination. Then along came this rank auteur (though Eric didn't actually employ the term), imposing his own idiosyncratic interpretation of the material. With many definitive images and singular representations that begged only confirmation of the director's tannic vision. Nothing had been left to Eric's own fledgling, sprouting imagination and that had been the problem. (Even though on this particular score, his imagination was neither fledgling nor sprouting, but rutted and grooved and fixed in a cicatrised vision all of its own).

From henceforth Eric devoted himself to rigorous study of film and its tropes. Though he continued to read works of imaginative fiction, rarely did they captivate and take possession of his soul as had the formative primer tale. The author of books was ever absent, but now their agent, his father, had also decamped and the cleft could not be closed. Rather the vast majority of his reading was about cinematic theory, the gaze of the audience viewer, the elements of montage and mise en scene. How the director chose to tell his story. The film director was ever present, spooring his imprint on every frame. Hitchcock even put himself in each one of his movies as an explicit acknowledgement of this. Every shadow, even the bloopers such as invasive umbral boom mics, pointed up the looming, contiguous manifestation of the accursed auteur.

And as an adult, Eric developed a career as a fierce and unstinting film critic, being particularly harsh on film adaptations of novels. That is to say, most films. He berated screenwriters for not coming up with their own stories, uniquely fashioned for the medium of celluloid. He lanced the ego of every film director who dared put himself at the forefront of the buzz around their own film. He delighted in pointing out the manipulation of sensibilities, the hidden emotional land mines directors sowed into their movies. People welcomed his schtick, the stick he used to beat jumped-up artists with. Even though few of them had read the novels and short stories these films were developed from, his audience also came to the conclusion that the director closed off too many possibilities for them to lie back and conjure up their own narratives between the scenes. More people read Eric's critiques than went to see the movies themselves. For his own part, Eric was so bored of writing by rote, the same pieces night after night after night.

Rescinderella

Cinderella had stamped Belinda for life. It's not especially obvious why this tale singularly resonated so deeply with her, setting her skeleton a hum and her brain all longingly desirous of merger. She herself wasn't persecuted by any siblings, ugly or otherwise. Her own mother was not in fact dead, never over-taxed her with chores, nor consigned her to rags for clothes. On the other hand, nor was Belinda herself interested in the finery of a ball gown, or a card-carrying cheerleader for the colour blue. While she didn't live in any grand style, nor hanker after it, neither did she feel particularly deprived, although the family home's imitation fireplace was most unsightly and didn't produce any cinders. More a sort of black charred powder scree from its faux coals. Mind you, chances are they were either carcinogenic, or would at least play merry hell with one's lungs.

Nor was she ostensibly awaiting rescue by any prince, be he charming or churlish. In point of fact, she actually felt rather shy in the presence of men. She wasn't possessed of any deep desire to close the intimacy gap and discover the horology of what made them tick. And she absolutely had no notion of what a foot fetishist might be, even though certain outré readings of the Cinderella tale could be interpreted in just such fashion.

Yet still the story spoke to her. In ungraspable, undefined terms, it just opened up her heart and nestled there. As Bruno Bettelheim advises us that fairy tales do, not that Belinda had read him. She felt whole whenever she conjured up a thought about Cinderella, even when they shared no dilemmas to probe together. Perhaps she associated with her heroine's isolation, but unlike her, it didn't really pose any particular threat to her mental wellbeing. Besides, when she was with Cinders, she was never truly alone anyway.

Came the day when she finally fledged from home by going to university. She almost blew her chances through changing her name by deed poll to Cindy, after she had already filled in her college application forms, which nearly made the system blow a gasket. Student Finance conceived of it as possible fraud, while the Senior Admissions Officer thought it might be a case of identity theft, motivated by an intent to groom. Fortunately, she was able to clear a path through the tangled tendrils of bureaucracy she had snaggled herself up in, despite not having read Kafka's *The Castle*, even though it was on her recommended reading list. The rechristening had been the first step on her journey to individuation, for she knew out in the real world, or as real as university ever approximates to the world, it would compel her to emerge from her cocoon. She was fully cognisant that her plunge into waters outside of her childhood home, offered her an opportunity to create herself anew. To discover who she really was. All was fluid and up for grabs. And from her limited palette, more of an inkwell really, she drew on her heroine Cinderella for indelibly inscribing her soul.

She closeted herself away in her digs with pen and paper and began to sketch out designs. She was to honour her nonesuch in ink. A tattoo to bind them together irrevocably and ineradicably. Skin sisters. The project seemed to be marked auspicious when she discovered a mouse in her room which she managed to catch and tame. Unaware that it was stricken with Lyme's Disease. A different, and less instantaneous, sort of transformation than that of a carriage-pulling horse or its coachman. Accordingly, her joints soon started to inflame and ache, though she put it down to pulling all-nighters doing her university work, to make up for her tattoo-design labours during the day. Though this ran counter to the rubicund rash on her cheeks, which were remarked on by friends as a sign of blushing good health.

Nevertheless, she pressed on like a trooper in her quest for self-elucidation. But her studies were starting to suffer as her student grant was diverted away from the course books on Victorian Literature, for brochures and catalogues of tattoo designs and glossy art books of the same. She kept the bars of the electric fire permanently switched off, as she huddled herself up to the hob boiling the lentils upon which she solely subsisted. But the sacrifices were requited, for after her in-depth researches, she resolved upon the full body-length adumbration of a spinal tattoo. And then in her 'eureka' moment, she hit upon the notion of a totem pole, constructed from all the totemic symbols derived from the story.

So, with the glass slipper as the fundament, erected upon it were the vitreous carriage, a pumpkin, two horses, a clock with its hands almost at midnight (synchronously echoing the close squeaks she'd had with getting her college essays in on deadline), two broomsticks to serve as its arms, all topped off with a mouse. She slapped her design down on the tattooist's glass counter. They discussed its minutiae and the pain range. Impatiently she accepted an appointment the next day to allow her a cooling-off period should she have a change of heart, which she thought an absolutely preposterous proposition. The man, though supposedly himself an artist, clearly couldn't see creative passion and fervour when it stood opposite glaring at him over a glass counter.

The pain was excruciating, but she gritted her way through it by telling herself that it represented the energy transference required of a metamorphosis. The larval her was finally transforming and flexing a butterfly's new-grown wings. When it was over, the tattooist gingerly guided her shuffling form over to a floor-length mirror. He took her through the stages of her tower there in amongst the bloodied, churned skin (which echoed the mutilation of Cinders' stepsisters' feet, as they tried to wedge their clodhopping plates into the chastisement of the cut glass crystal slipper). She felt so powerful, she didn't even resort to holding up the paper robe to mask her frontal nudity presenting to him, as she swivelled her neck to view her dorsal depiction in the looking glass.

Unfortunately, the needles hadn't been terribly clean. She was infected with hepatitis and possibly other germs that tainted her blood. Out-blasting even her worsening Lyme's Disease that had a head's start on these Johnny-come-lately pathologies. Rather than take to the wing, she had emerged apterous from her puparium. Now her research was devoted to her own symptoms, throughout every online portal in the kingdom and beyond. None matched and yet every last one of them fit her to a T. Or a glass slipper for that matter. Often she fell asleep in front of the electric fire, so drained was she by her labours. Accordingly, flyaway coils of her hair were singed, while holes were burned into her clothes which she was increasingly less inclined to change out of into fresh raiment.

She died before the invitations for the summer ball to mark the end of the academic year landed in students' pigeon holes. The autopsy mirrored the mélange of elements in the composition of the tattoo on her anterior, until she was stitched back up again. Her parents had to fight tooth and nail not to be held liable for her unredeemed student loan, given that she was endowed with no future earning power through being deceased, rather than having just turned into a post-exam pumpkin. In their baffled pique they had her cremated, though they declined the firm of Aarne, Thompson, and Uther's catalogued prod of a cut-glass urn. Truly she had fused into Cinders, only in an oven rather than any crystal carriage.

Collateral Thinking

Rishi was an only child. His parents both worked tremendously long hours. But it wasn't only their time they were miserly with in respect of their son. Since nor did they compensate for their insufficiency by fringing him with a mound of toys to eke out his lonely afternoons, when he came home from school to an empty house. Nor books to engage his imagination. The only stories in this house sat between staircases. For his part, Rishi couldn't settle to the mediated ministrations of an inanimate nanny, since he found television cartoonish, even when enacted by live human actors.

Surrounded in the main only by himself, he invented games to play. And in inventing games he didn't so much as invent rules, but narratives. Bottle caps became planets, milk tops flying saucers (non-aligned scale was dismissed from being a problem). Discarded carrot tops were reclaimed from the bin and became desert islands with palm trees. When after several days service in the oceans of his imagination, their decaying rot was absorbed into the narrative as pollution's blight, Rishi waving their aluminium foil birds off, as they flew to new lands beyond cotton wool clouds without being weighed down by the coagulated fat of cooked meat juices. He created circuses from bathroom detritus, trapezes and high wires from dental floss, cotton ear buds to steady the balance of the intrepid funambulists. He fashioned pirate ships, gladiatorial amphitheatres, hospitals and zoos. Castles besieged by horse-borne knights with their tooth-pick lances, leading armies of safety-pin archers, while elastic band ballistas fired peas against the battlements. But whatever the setting spawned by his precocious ingenuity, it was the dialogue that sprung from the scenarios which drove the stories. He was adept at simultaneously holding multifarious characters and their diverse motivations with ease. His voice might not yet possess much range, but the characters were still clearly delineated one from another by their idiolect.

On one occasion when the family had been uprooted to an aunt's house for a family wedding, Rishi had found himself bereft of prompts even more than usual in the immaculately maintained mansion. He was still further at an utterly loose end while the adults were off toasting the happy event at a restaurant. He noticed that for all the spotlessness of his aunt's interiors, there was one slight frayed thread. Or several. The lounge carpet that had recently played host to so many shod feet, had in places been scuffed and bobbled and blistered. Gingerly he lay down on the rich ply and plucked at a loose billow of the woof. It came away easily enough and he rolled it between the tip of finger and thumb as his imagination whirred as to what entity he might cast it into.

He proceeded to tug several more flocculent filaments and compressed them together into indeterminate blobs.

He made four of these and a smaller one to serve as the ball and proceeded to play an impromptu game of two-a-side football. The legs of a low-lying table served for the goals, while he perched himself prone on his stomach just outside the field of play to wield his fluffy players. Again, the key element was the commentary he provided. Four of the best footballers in the world, having an intricate nexus of family histories spun for them in greater detail than their own ghostwriters could have provided, albeit less hagiographical.

He was enjoying a most satisfying game tantalisingly poised at 17-17, when he heard the sound of voices outside the front door. In his haste he banged his head on the table as he scooped up his fuzzballers and stashed them in his pocket. With the key turning in the lock, he quickly surveyed the carpet to ensure he had not been over-vigorous in his threshing of fibre and was satisfied that there were no evident patches of baldness where his reaping had occurred. Indeed, his aunt congratulated him with a kiss into his hair on being such a good boy in their absence, his uncle had commented that he must have a great facility for entertaining himself, while his parents looked sheepish as if they'd forgotten all about him even being left behind there as they had wined and dined. His uncle gave him a banknote and he stuffed it in his pocket, grazing his furballs as he did so. His Dad made an asinine remark about how Rishi could now probably afford that toy he had always wanted, when Rishi knew there to be no such thing. He didn't possess a clue what he might do with the money. Perhaps he would invest in a piggy bank, but that seemed somewhat of a forlorn ambition, since all the money would go on the infrastructure, when there was unlikely to be further deposits needing recourse of it.

Yet the incident had stirred something in his father. He felt a tad guilty at being so distanced from his son. So one surprising afternoon of a weekend, when instead of retiring for a nap to recharge energies depleted by the working week, he offered to join his son down on the floor to participate in his game. Rishi was dubious at first, but awed at the uniqueness of the circumstance, swiftly relented and invited his father to manoeuvre the garage-cum-carpark accessories around the tiled floor with him. After initially protesting his old bones having to fold themselves in order to attain floor level, he then remarked on the frigidness of the surface and airily tossed out a vague warning about developing arthritis in chilled bones. Yet to Rishi it was unclear if his father was addressing himself, or whether it was directed to him who after all, spent day after day exposed to such conditions.

His father picked up one of Rishi's recycled items. It was the safety plastic from one of his own disposable razors. He stared at his son long and hard before calmly explaining that such shields were important not only from a safety aspect, but also it kept the blades of his razors from becoming corroded and discoloured by exposure to air. Rishi defended himself by saying both razor and shield had already been discarded into the bathroom bin and he had merely availed himself of the plastic in order to make a ramp to stop vehicles passing the lowered barrier (a broken pencil housed in a glob of plasticine) without paying their ticket at the booth (an empty lipstick outer tube standing vertical on its square base).

His father pursed his brow at the thought of his son rummaging through bins, but declined to voice his distaste for reasons he himself was not entirely clear on. He proceeded to pick up and examine another instrument of the game. A box of matches came away from the four variegated ointment lids that functioned as wheels to its chassis. Father brought the matchbox up to his ear and shook it to establish that it was empty. Fortunately, he was not one of those smokers who placed his used matches back in the box to confound the issue. He inquired where Rishi had come by the ointment tops, since he could not credit that his three-handed family had simultaneously finished four tubes of emollient, for them all to end up together in the bin. His temples wrinkled at the prospect of having to replace all four in the weekly shop. Rishi tried to salve his father's concern, that no, the balsams and demulcents were all still operative, he had merely borrowed their caps for the duration of today's play session. Again his father chided him about untrammelled access for oxygen, in this case to harden the various lotions and creams inside, thus likely to prevent their transmission through the shaft, or out through the spout if caked and congealed there. Rishi looked at the four wheels denuded of their chassis and offered to go replace them instantly. His father demurred, heart-struck at the plaintive note in his son's words. Here he was offering to join the garage forecourt game, when in fact his critical mien was on the brink of converting it into a breaker's scrapyard. Just this once, Rishi could play with the lids, if he secured a vow from his son that he would not prematurely seize upon anything that was still in service. Rishi eagerly nodded assent and took the matchbox from his father to reconstitute his car. The narrative being that it had been in the repair shop, despite it more having the look to his father's eye of a chop-shop product, though surely Rishi knew nothing of such nefarious agencies? In truth his whole play world seemed to be one large chop-shop. But at least it appeared to be a happy, safe and trustworthy one.

Or it had been, until invaded and inspected by his father in his impromptu health and safety guise. For next he picked up a strange looking object, like a mini-cigar case even though on the odd occasion he himself indulged in a cigar, he would always opt for a Havana rather than a Perfecto. Moreover, this was a shabby plastic tube rather than fashioned from impermeable metal and lacked for any identifying branding. His father quizzed him as to what such an object was, to which Rishi automatically offered up its representational identity of an air pump for cars to be able to re-inflate their tyres. His father sputtered his disbelief and tried to correct his son's misconstruing of the question. It was at that moment that Rishi seriously reconsidered his decision to accede to his dad's request to come down to his level and join in. His car-owning father surely knew what a garage looked like, how its many features operated. Yet here he was acting no different to an extra-terrestrial who had just landed on earth for the very first time. He was clearly too much of a literalist and they hadn't even started the game in earnest yet. It was true that in previous sessions such an object had lent itself even more perfectly to making a rocket ship, but he ventured that his father's imagination clearly wouldn't have been sufficiently lithe to have made that association either. This was the nature of the play beast, the retelling of stories necessarily differed on each recreation, due to the found objects available.

Rishi affirmed that it had indeed, been yet another item salvaged from the bathroom bin, but his father still scratched his head and stroked his chin while twirling the vessel around in his fingers. His wife happened to amble into the room, so he rose from his stiffening sprawl and flourished the item in her face and asked her if she knew what it was their son was playing with. She blanched a tad before inclining to whisper in his ear. The husband looked quizzical and asked her what an 'applicator' was exactly. Again she brought her mouth up to his ear, shrouded it with her cupped hand in order to give him a longer exposition. The cartridge shot from his hands and narrowly missed Rishi's head. His father was wiping his hands against his shirt and then wildly shaking them at the wrist, blowing on his fingers as if they were burning. So his father had finally contributed, but again had endowed the scenario hopelessly wrong. He had configured the thing as a space rocket rather than an air inflator after all and then launched it at the garage entailing calamitous conflagration. Well, rockets need fuel as well he supposed, trying to restitch his narrative stream back together.

His father began to harangue him about wallowing around in filth and dirt. Rishi wasn't sure quite what he was referring to. His father's foot swept towards him and levelled his jerry-built garage. Then he squatted down to his haunches, scooping up the lotion tops, the razor shield, the foil sheet that had housed headache tablets but now in the garage represented a box for spare car parts. The sundry world of his garage exuding from between his father's clenched fingers, was brandished vehemently towards Rishi, save for the applicator which remained forlornly on the floor. Half air-inflator, half rocket ship, wholly shunned. With spittle-laden emphasis, his father was expostulating about germs and disease and infection. Rishi was no longer to trawl through the house's bins and remove items from them. Now Rishi exploded, demanding his father and mother buy him some proper toys instead. The pair of them didn't seem to be going without, to judge by the plethora of beauty ointments, the cigar smoking, the wine bottle corks, Mama's applicator thingy. His mother spluttered that was hardly a luxury item, but Rishi went on with his litany of cast-off packaging he had been forced to press into service as toys.

His parents took his complaints on board. It actually seemed a reasonable rate of exchange to prevent him rooting in the bins. And they really did love their son and heir. However, the moulded plastic toys and games that emerged from cardboard boxes with garish depictions on their covers, failed to engage and spark his imagination as had the trove of more humble jetsam. Never again was he able to recapture such wondrous narratives and his choral dialogues fell silent.

Teratological

Most kids who imbibe fairy tales are able to side with the protagonist and follow them doggedly all the way through to a ready acceptance of the tail/tale wagging happy ending. Let's face it, the fairy story realm is hardly one playing host to internecine jungle warfare summoning an agent orange air strike. At best the dark forest presents no more than an innocuous assault course for the hero/heroine to navigate. A few fallen logs to wobble-balance across. Some tendrils to climb and maybe swing over a sunken depression in the leaf litter. The gingerbread house doesn't sit behind a ten foot wall to be scaled now does it? The minotaurhetorical device at the heart of the maze, is ever on a hiding to nothing. A mere jack-in-the-box to leap out and go boo! In order to shuffle the hero over into the beatific denouement of his/her destiny. Yet there are a few jittery outliers who cannot get beyond the obstacular in the labyrinth, to wit the dragon, the big bad wolf, the man-eating giant, the wicked witch. Anything with an outsized overbite.

The monstrous images stay with them. Looming larger in their imaginations than the scale of menace they were intended to represent in the original story, only these never wither away. The horrors unharnessed. Beasts not bested. Rather they remain in residence under the bed. They possess the night, inhabiting shadows and unexplained noises. They are utterly persecutory and sinister. Mummy can't see them no matter how many times the child compels her to look in the wardrobe. Irrespective of how frequently Daddy flicks on the switch, they are never frozen in the searchlight. And when Daddy is gone again, the lamb lies there staring up at the extinguished bulb, imagining it the glass escape hatch of his oubliette where he is condemned to flinch and tremble in the presence of his unseen tormentors. Such children are thus marked for life by these dreads. It wholly determines their temper. Forever looking over their shoulder. Scared of their own and others' shadows. Perpetually on the back foot, ready to turn tail and run, rather than look life in the eye. Wounded. Panopticised by their own dreads.

Were their parents wrong to read them such formative tales? Had they not carried out a proper risk assessment? Were they so ignorant of their own issue's mental make-up, as to miscalculate the likely affect of introducing the possibility of such chimera? How could the parent cop the blame when the unformed child's psyche is still such a roiling sea of the inchoate? How could they possibly predict their child's quavering predisposition? Did either of them suffer such preformationary terrors? If they can't recall, then they almost certainly didn't. Who is to say what is premature and what isn't in terms of the existence of evil? Or rank badness at least. Whatever the genetic inheritance, such is this literary nurture that confirms, or peradventure confers, their life of troubledness and disquiet.

And whither the fate of this quailing cohort once it reaches the age of majority? Having at least sloughed off the fear of bursting out of their own childish bones into fully fledged adulthood. That it was merely an incremental evolution, rather than an all-enveloping transmutation as per fairy stories. But in one respect they do undergo a morphological change, prodded by their hyper-vigilance. They become multi-lensed. Since they constantly survey news reports and stories for threats. They collect data, calculate probabilities, triangulate ominous geometries back to themselves. Draw up portentous narratives. They become Argus-eyed, with myriad compound screens and monitor lenses like the humble fly. So many ocular apertures, yet none are the Third Eye, or any of the higher Buddhist realms of insight and spiritual calm. Rather they are mirrors, reflecting and telescopically multiplying their terrors back to them hundredfold. Nor are they ever all switched off and shuttered blank at the same time, but instead, endlessly revolve their sentry duty. These preternaturally alert beings prefer the nighttime to that of day. Despite darkness being the crucible of their primal fears, they feel more comfortable within its parameters, since they have perennially occupied its every waking minute. They know its dimensions. Its limited palette of shades and hues. They can more readily detect the slightest motion, prompting their reflexive response of recoiling and hurtling away out of its clutches. There is just too much pother by day. Too many untrustworthy saturations of light, too broad a sweep of its spectrum, to know where they stand within it.

The typical jobs they do are night watchmen, looking over banks of CCTV monitors. Or other cheap-rate electricity, data-crunching jobs in seclusion. Isolated and alone, but again it makes them feel more at home. For though they might prefer allies in their campaign to keep the teratological at bay, they cannot trust to anybody else's true colours. They took Little Red Riding Hood's wolf to heart and inscribed it there, in blood and gristle. Never would they allow themselves to be taken in by nice old grannies in rocking chairs. Nor seemingly redemptive woodsmen bearing giant axes. Well might they care for some romance to rescue them from their self-created cage, but the transformation of the frog into a prince scares them too much. For to their mind, again it would necessitate themselves suffering the most terrible of transmogrifications and the thought just shatters their being. They cannot dare embrace any such fantasy.

It soon develops into a self-reinforcing isolation anyway. As they become more and more focused on the external threat, they begin to neglect their own inner substance. Their posture becomes stooped and hunched as the spine melds itself to the curvature of their monitoring chair. Their nails grow long and taloned, despite their daily dance across keyboards, while their hair grows lank and matted as it goes unwashed. They are even further shunned by a society that views them as truly monstrous.

Pentimento Mori

This story has no words. No, that's not right of course. This story is told without words. No, that's not quite it either. Not that this story is beyond words. This story demands to be told because that's what it's about. A need to be told. To be furnished with full information. This story is therefore about unspoken words. Yes that's it. This story is about the unspoken. It's about ellipsis. Actually it's about more than that. Emptiness. Dirty great voids. This is a story about silence. Hush now and listen up.

Martin had a twin. Many people do. But unlike most cases, this is not a tale of pre-parturition preterition. Martin's was carried along to term along with him. Although his twin didn't last too long out of the womb, albeit tarrying just enough to be conferred with a name. It was about a month or so, until he was carried off by some infant infection long-ere deemed to have been licked by superior hygiene and nutrition. Naturally Martin had been equally exposed to the same short-stay mother's milk and sanitation regimen, yet he had not succumbed to any disease. Not that he was aware of any of this plainly, still being in the stage of making his rods and cones cohere into settled vision and beginning to discern a face or two. Maybe he *had* clocked his brother, but the memory engrams were even further behind in maturation and he retained no abiding image of him. Even if he had, Jacques Lacan might have attributed it to the mirror stage of development, though that usually didn't kick in until six months of age. Anyway, it was all moot. Extending even to the very existence of his brother, since the second Moses basket was scuttled in the local village pond; half the babygros were returned to Mothercare still sealed in their plastic; the double buggy traded in for a simple single, and so on and so forth. In hindsight, all these negotiations must have involved an airing of the decedent reason why they were being returned. Before the antecedent was once and for all hammered into its airless tomb.

The de-brotherisation had been so comprehensive that Martin was never aware of his twin's former distinct existence, even when he was able to distinguish his own face from that of other people and a sad countenance from a happy one. The latter having proved a surpassingly hard task to master, since his parents failed miserably to model what a happy face looked like. They had, perhaps not unreasonably, taken the death of his brother very hard. His mother bore her grief inside, while his father went out and raged against the world. They did not face their loss together, in any united, mutually supportive way. It drove them apart, though in the claustrophobic space of their spacious home, they actually rather cramped one another inordinately. Even ensconced in separate rooms within the house, it was as if their pneumas slipped the leash of their physical bodies, crept through the crack under the door and drifted purposefully until able to colonise its spouse and afflict their grieving presence. Importuning them that they were mourning in the wrong way.

And inevitably, in such a brooding atmosphere he was swept up in the stewing ferment. When his parents did actually coincide in the same space, such as over the table at meal times, Martin became the focus of their wrangling. There was no question of both parents' love for him. Perhaps all the more, in the light of his brother's premature subtraction from the family circle that had collapsed one side of a square to dispose a triangle. But their love was always defined in terms of the missing limb. He should have been showered with a combined fifty percent of their love, but now was the recipient of the brunt of the full dose. And then some over and above to indemnify. Their entire focus was around his wellbeing, which was not the same as his thriving.

His father had interpreted his brother's demise as being down to inherent physical weakness and strove to avoid a cognate fate for the twin that had survived him. His mother had adopted an irreconcilable approach, being highly overprotective to ensure that no ill befell him. She undertook an elaborate child-proofing of the house, with a myriad of cushions and pillows padding the walls, table legs and unit corners trussed up in bubble wrap and foam, every potential sharp angle and edge smoothed off and blunted. The father accused her of suffocating the child, not allowing him to breathe, let alone allowing him to roam and receive his inuring share of knocks and bruises. She rounded on him and lambasted that if that was the case, why had he so readily agreed *not* to tell him about the whilom existence of his brother? For what was the rationale there, if not to protect his fragile psyche from a crushing, overwhelming blow? Of course, neither could refer directly to what each viewed as the clinching evidence of their case; how the painstaking intricacy applied to securing each room in the house, was mirrored in the unadorned load-bearing wall of their joint silence which ran throughout the interior.

In point of indubitable fact, on the general smothering mother issue, the father was invalid (and why might anyone expect anything else from a person who perpetually raged against the unfairness of the world?) For when he was out of the house peevish and seething at work, she was actually too depressed to spend any time in the room with her son. Leaving him plenty free to go waddling on solo squabbed excursions and wadding-buffered explorations. The house may have been enveloped and swaddled, but Martin wasn't, which would in due course lead to the downfall of this particular house of husher.

Ordinarily, the entirety of this passed over the young child's head. Both the contentious and lacklustre parenting he was exposed to, but also its very source in the once fugacious existence of a sibling. And yet Martin himself was not entirely without sensation. Indescribable feelings, which may have been in part due to continued poor modelling on this score by his parents; or by humanity as a species, since these particular impressions are perhaps yet to have accurate words ascribed to them by scientists, artists or paranormalists. For he was experiencing something missing. A hollow. A fissure. A bloody great chasm. Sometimes in his stomach, other times like a gouge in his side. The Roman soldier's spear sunk into Christ's flank had nothing on him. With no frame of reference, he imagined these just to be the foibles of his corporeality as it grew and burst through its previous cellular structural mosaic.

Not that this stripling sprout would have put it in quite those words. It didn't hurt, yet he was in pain. A dull ache, like a hunger or a constant heavy-headedness. He could function quite properly and move on through it, but he also felt as if he didn't want to. Tangibly the reverberations of his body were trying to tell him something, but he couldn't tune into their non-linguistic wavelength. It was downgraded to white noise in an era when a digital world had dispensed with the phenomena. There were still shipping forecasts to warn of oncoming storms on long wave, but the trigonometric ports of call were thought of as bygone these days.

It was on one of his unaided navigations around the house at age nine, when he discovered the family sepulchre. Or a piece of paper with the glimmers of a trace of a map to its location at least. 'X' marks the spot for someone excised from this life. It was a bill from a cemetery for grave tending, stone cleaning and upkeep. There was a name, 'William –', someone who evidently bore the same patronymic as he himself. It couldn't have been either Gramps or Pop-Pop, since they were both still alive and valiantly trying to fill the puncture in the parenting dyke by filling up the cavity breach with sweets and chocolate and outings to Pop-Pop's allotment. It couldn't have been Nanna of course, for even though he didn't know her actual given cognomen, 'William' was clearly a male name. An uncle perhaps, but then why were his parents charged with the responsibility of care for an expired uncle? They must really have loved the man. Yet them loving anybody was hard to conceive and triangulate. It was only when he had fully perused the document that he disinterred the biggest clue yet. The word 'infant' appended to the size column. His hand reflexively moved to his side to try and absorb and absolve the shooting pain there.

Though abating, the sting did not entirely disappear for the rest of the day. It put paid to further expeditionary forays, so he sat in his room trying to tease out more co-ordinates from the uncharted paper. But no more formulas translated their abstruse lore unto him. Instead he waited until dinner time, whereupon he proceeded to pre-empt the usual running order of heavily agenda-ised un-minuted items between his parents, by smoothing the maintenance bill on the table and drumming a pointed finger down on it. His parents swapped looks, before his father sank his head to the table. It wasn't entirely clear whether the words unblocked the tears, or the tears unblocked the words, but both came out in a spurt. Martin sat there impassively, other than the clenching of fists at the end of his arms outstretched on the table. Both parents tried to reach across for Martin's hands to embrace one each, but he retracted them sharply and held them rigidly to his sides like a self-made straitjacket, even though the contact pressure increased the throbbing pain raging there. His father rose from the table and tried to hug him, but Martin shucked him off. It was beginning to make sense to him. The twin-shaped hollowness, the fraternal-sized gape in his side. Where he should have been cloven together with his twin, he had been cloven apart.

When his parents ran out of the stamina to utter any more expiating words, Martin finally passed his judgement on them. "So all this time that I've had to bear your craziness on my own? When I could have had an ally, someone to split the load with?"

"Well no darling, your brother died before he could become your, well, ally."

"But he's here, with me, inside. Only I never knew

what his presence was."

"Well that's simply fantastic that you can feel him like that. We unfortunately can't."

"Because you killed him."

"We didn't darling, the illness –"

"No, you bricked him up and smothered his memory. And in doing so you hollowed me out and throttled my ability to breathe too."

A lacuna you see. They did manage to find a word to describe the physical sensation he was feeling after all.

Broken Shards of Pottery

"You don't want your head filled with myth and magic and other such nonsense. You want something that's going to set you up properly for knowing about the world you're growing up in. How we arrived here. So I'm going to read you a book all about history. A chapter each night to usher you off into sleep."

And so Kevin's father did just that. A thick book covering world history from the earliest grave-borne evidence of civilisations, all the way through two great World Wars and culminating in the Cold War. He did so with drab and uninflected voice, serving only as a metronomic drone to lull Kevin into drowsiness. Thus each night, though striving manfully to stay awake as he did, Kevin slipped under into the land of nod. His father never looked up from the compendium to notice his son was no longer attentively digesting each night's exposition of events from the past.

Yet there were an awful lot of chapters to get through. So that though Kevin missed out on lots of information, he also imbibed much before he succumbed to chronologically induced slumber. Enough for him to start discerning patterns and repetitions. Of Oriental despotism and Occidental dynastic jealousies. Of Caesars, Kaisers, Chiefs, Emperors, Czars, Tsars, Shahs, Kings, (the odd Queen here and there), Sultans, Emirs, Khans, Maharajahs, Mikados and Caliphs. Snobs, sociopaths, paranoids, Messiah-complexers, all with their wars and dreams of empire. Of ever-shifting borders and discovery of new territories. Of class conflict. Generational oedipal conflict. Of oedipal class conflicts. So that although the precise context was fractured each time he passed over into sopor, in fact the narrative was easily picked up the next night as unchanged and unchanging, other than the names and the dates. He never got beyond Morpheus' waiting room, never had to offer up any entry toll, since his nights were dreamless. For his father had managed to perfectly quash any fantasy life brewing in his unconscious. Instead it was populated with a dreary litany of death and ambition, which in its relentlessness proved surprisingly untroubling so as not to stir any anxieties in him. However, by day he was no closer to unlocking the mysteries as to how the world had attained its present anxiety-ridden, parlous state.

But came the peremptory evening, when his father snapped shut the hard cover with a squelch against the thick wedge of pages for the final time. All caught up to the carpet bombing, nuclear holocausts, genocides and kamikaze suicides of the Second World War. By now Kevin was old enough to prop open his eyelids sufficiently long, to secure a later bedtime and also able to persevere through his father's bombination and stay awake throughout. He asked his father what they were going to read next. "Well that was just a broad overview, so I thought we'd focus in a little more keenly on the history closest to ourselves. To that end we're going to read Thomas Babington Macaulay's *The History Of England* in five volumes. In addition to being an excellent study of Britain's evolution to attain an unrivalled supremacy throughout the world, the language is rich and a delight in its own right. You won't need to read Dickens or Trollope, or even perish the thought George Eliot. Macaulay can match them all. Lie back and luxuriate in his language lad."

It was hard for Kevin to align Macaulay's Whiggish view of the inevitable progress of history; of the move from absolute monarchs towards Prime Ministers, Presidents, Chancellors and Taoiseachs, when set against his previous unalloyed diet of war, grudges and petty politicking from on high. None of this new breed seemed particularly immune or averse to shedding the blood of the citizens in whose names they nominally ruled. And as for the sumptuous language, it was tough to bask in any prose seeped in his father's lisping sibilance. Out of curiosity he went to the school library and read Dickens, Trollope and Eliot. The two men he found to be reportage with a bit of literary gloss, so just more historical tidings really. The main revelation with Eliot was that he was a she. Beyond that mild wonder, the fustian first page of *Middlemarch* augured a level of hardship at least twice that suffered by Mao Tse-Tung on his Long March, so Kevin deferred, permanently. Seemed like his father was correct on the literature score at least. Which was vaguely troubling in itself. So instead he started reading Macaulay under his own auspices, just to see if his father's boasts on behalf of the man's literary abilities held up. He wasn't sure, as to his way of thinking, he seemed no less fruity than the august stylists of fiction. But now he found himself ahead of his father's progress through the book at his bedside each evening. History was repeating itself with a syncopated echo. And the same dynamic afflicted his school history lessons. He already knew everything they were studying, because he'd had it read to him. History began to seem arid. It bored him because he'd heard it all before. Literally and through discerning its repetitive nature.

Instead he sat in school attempting to figure out exactly how history spoke to his own day and age. After all, that was the promise held out to him by his father at the very outset of this never-ending endeavour. He tried to plot the exact lines of transmission, the inheritances, the slowly changing values, when grievances surfaced and why they might be held in check until they burst forth (clearly they never fully disappeared, no matter how long they remained latent as the ethnic cleansing in Yugoslavia and the tribal genocide in Rwanda showed him nightly on the news). But the task proved largely intractable. He tried importing his small amount of knowledge of statistical analysis from mathematics and fluid dynamics from physics to help him in his quest, but he concluded that history did not lend itself to scientific method in any single degree. (A later splensplifferous discussion at university with a physicist would partly modify this belief, as he learned of Chaos Theory and more specifically the functioning of The Butterfly Effect). He boned up on pop psychology, to try and discern how Stalin's paranoia and George III's porphyria might have impacted their momentous decisions that shaped historical events. But again the task defeated him. The scale of agency within history was ungraspable. Like war reportage when embedded journalists and observers can only give eye witness to one tiny part of the battlefield, purblind to what was going on elsewhere along the front.

When it came time to make his final subject selections for A-Level study as a precursor to university, he took the path of least resistance. History naturally, since the syllabus was such a breeze for him. Next, perhaps in spite of himself and certainly to spite his father's philistinism, he plumped for English, to see if he could be guided into conceiving how great works of literature could speak to him, seeing as he had been unable to secure just such through his own initiatives. Unfortunately however, there was no escaping an engagement with George Eliot this time round, since she was one of the examined texts. Finally he opted for Economics, simply because half of the course work comprised Economic History, which he also reckoned he had down pat. Economics, another cross-current pull on great events and movements, that one was obliged to add into the historical mix. One that Karl Marx said out-trumped all others and rendered them nugatory. Even though Five Year Plans owed more to Stalin and Mao's individual madness than sound economic principles. Henry Ford could have taught them a thing or two about productivity. The man who proclaimed 'history is more or less bunk'. Shame he was a nutter of the highest order too.

Having deftly piloted his way through the stress and pressure of A-Levels by minimising his workload, (George Eliot aside which had proved a predictable slog), he had achieved the offer of studying History at the most prestigious of British universities. His father was so proud, silently and not so silently giving himself a pat on the back for setting his son up so well early in life, through his choice of nourishment for the burgeoning grey matter. To mark his son's attainment, his father went to a renowned auction house (staffed entirely by alumni from the most prestigious of British universities) and outbid the field for an original King's pardon of some scurrilous knave, with two-thirds of the royal seal still intact. He had it framed in heavy glass before presenting this real piece of history to Kevin with great pomp and ceremony, albeit within the unpalatial setting of the family parlour. But to his great pain, his son was completely unmoved by the artefact. He could not be impressed upon either to take it with him to university, (admittedly it was an unwieldy thing to cart about on a train), nor would Kevin permit it to be mounted on his bedroom wall at home in his absence. For him history was prosaic, what could demonstrably be proved to have happened. It needed no sphragistic gilding, no symbolic totemising. And for all his father's dusting off his superannuated schoolboy Latin in order to translate the royal proclamation, it was left to him rather than Kevin, to spend his leisure time vainly trying to establish whether the named varlet had indeed walked free of the gibbet or not. But as Kevin could have told him, the early Restoration historical record was somewhat patchy. Instead Kevin packed up his resolutely modern possessions and granted himself a common or garden pardon to take his leave from the suburban kingdom of his parents.

Fairly swiftly Kevin realised that even at this forge of the finest minds making history through research and academic publishing, there was little more to be learned. Manifold original documents lay in the university library, delivered with rubber gloves and perused on wooden lecterns. Library stacks teeming with works of microscopic detail on any and every historical period or theme one could anticipate. And Kevin could anticipate more than most.

But other than that, little else to stretch his interest. No new great ideas under a sun blotted out by the venerable cupola of the university library. In his first lecture on general historical principles, he was advised that the evidence was the evidence, but its interpretation could only be properly made by entering the empathic matrix of the people of the time under study. It was rank bad history to impose our values and judgements on the people of the past. But Kevin had no desire to step back in order to enter the mind of a Jacobite or a Sans-Culotte, so his form neither lightened nor darkened the door of the Humanities' new modern lecture block again, although the building was environmentally controlled for both light and temperature anyway. From this point on, Kevin was all about the here and now. Drinking, lechering and general absorption in the principle of pleasure. Empirical, but decidedly not pedagogic.

Though he turned in unenthusiastic and uninspired essays, he wasn't entirely an irredeemable wastrel. Instead he used his privilege of free time to try and write his own fiction, to put to right the shortcomings, as he saw it, of the classic canon of literature that he had wrestled with unsuccessfully. The great novel, he determined, had to interrogate the world around us. But to do so it must not draw upon the tortured, tangled web of historical conditions as to how it had arrived there. For as he well knew, that tillage was fallow and infecund and would blunt or even snap any inky harrow. Yet he was no more successful in his own creative efforts, continually becoming stymied in his attempts to establish a true contemporaneity to his writing. History always intruded, events and feelings welled from the past. References very quickly became outdated and consigned to history. The moment one typed 'The End' on a manuscript, you bookended its development and the clock started ticking on dragging the text back into the folds of time. History was the collective result of innumerable actors and forces shaping events. Trying to draw out a single protagonist and a sprinkling of other characters for the focus of a novel, proved nigh on impossible. They were always sucked back into the greater context. The problem with the English novel he decided, was that it could not prevent itself from becoming infected with the bacillus of history. And even that metaphor, which itself should have been derived from scientific terms, was associated with history and the great plague. What was required was a Year Zero to sweep away the past, but again, not only was that specific to a historical epoch, but Year Zero by necessity develops into year one, two and so on.

He naturally veered towards science-fiction in his writing, as then he could fracture and fragment linear time. But the use of prolepsis, deja-vu, parallel universes with alternate realities and other dizzying time slips, left his beta reader pals confused. Worse, one of them accused him of teleology, the very worst charge that could be hurled at a historian, let alone someone dabbling in literature. He knew the endpoint where he wanted his story to arrive, but it cast too giant a shadow over the entirety that preceded it. Confound it, perhaps the Whiggish spirit of Macaulay had seeped into him and colonised his very marrow after all.

The exams at the end of his freshman year came at a bad time. He had consigned his great novel to the bin, thwarted at every turn in trying to eliminate the role of the past in shaping current narratives. His posh girlfriend had also just dumped him after a row about the ahistoricality of Marie Antoinette ever having said "Let them eat brioche", prompted initially by him serving up an afternoon tea from a hotplate high-street bakers, rather than an artisanal patisserie. Having done no exam revision might not have hobbled him as it might others and besides, the first paper was for general principles and posed the unvarnished question, 'Why History?' which he attacked with unbridled relish. He composed a diatribe against the discipline, reasoning that knowing one's history did not leave mankind better prepared to avoid the mistakes of the past; one never knew quite which bit of history was going to repeat itself when. As The Butterfly Effect suggested, a tiny alteration in the starting conditions could lead to wildly divergent outcomes from a seemingly similar past set of circumstances. Then there was the problem of the partial nature of evidence. History was written by the winners, or their propagandists and apologists at least, Shakespeare being a prime example. The further back you went, the more partial the historical record, with women, peasants, slaves and great swathes of society excluded and unrepresented from having their versions of history told. Next to take into account, was the role of the market and academia in forging history. No one wants to read a book arguing the same things as a previous academic publication. So professional historians have to carve out new untrodden seams, either taking an obtusely contrary position on an accepted historical theory, or researching an unchartered and inevitably obscure new furrow. Then they make the evidence back up their viewpoint, through whatever partisan skewed selection of the already incomplete record they can muster. Additionally, historians no matter how much they protest, are not purely objective. Most have political agendas. Reactionary or Progressive, either inclination could argue their case for a historical period simply by moving the dates under examination. A mere shift of dates by thirty years one way could prove the triumph of progressivism and reform, or thirty years the other way asserts a consummate period of conservatism resisting any change. Who reads Macaulay anymore anyway? Certainly no one in this university.

He was asked by his tutors to quit his degree and leave at the end of his first year. Well, not 'asked' so much as 'demanded', Norman French outranking Anglo-Saxon English. And not just rustication, but being sent down back into the bowels of suburbia. He protested, calling them jobsworths, feather-bedded through secure tenure. Scoliotics rather than scholiasts, cringingly spineless in the face of a well-argued critique. They asked him how many research papers and publications he'd brought out, even as they doffed their mortar boards in his direction, mockingly soliciting a donation. They were indeed ensconced in their posts for life, while he had not lasted a full year. He excoriated them all as revisionists, to which they countered that if only he himself had been the slightest bit of a revisionist and worked for his exams, who knows what he might have achieved for a grade? From the entrance exam and interview, they had earmarked him for the student who would most likely be taken into their academic ranks down the line, but his flouting of tradition had done for him. He pronounced them all anachronistic in the greatest of anachronistic institutions that had outlived its nine-hundred years' existence, then beat his retreat. Catapulted out into the big wide world with no qualifications, no means of support, and no great English novel to his name, he had no choice but to return home. His broken-hearted father did not offer to tuck him in his bed and read history books to him, which was just as well, since he would probably have re-enacted any of countless historical incidents of defenestration. His inquiry on the QT, of the worth of his King's Pardon, only suggested that his old man had been palmed off with a fake. Par for the historical course.

Tempera Tantrum

The steam had ceased swirling from her hot drink, even though it was no longer being used as a meditative well-spring. Instead she was lost in the newspaper's Quizword, though she hadn't filled in an answer for the entire period it took the coffee to cool. She had merely craved time to tune out, to be away from the unadulterated juvenile company of her daughter. To that end, she had first busied herself in the overelaborate task flow of brewing coffee in a cafetière. The sort of fluid and pressure dynamics of Physics that had perennially baffled her at school, but which had proven of such utility to contrive a 'time-out' at work when she had needed to take a mental breather. But shorn of the hide of her job, replaced by the pelage of motherhood, she further augmented the time and motionless of an untouched coffee, by emptying the dregs of the grains, rinsing and washing the cafetière and inverting it to dry on the draining board. But after that rigmarole had all been played out, she still wanted to further eke out this interlude. To stretch and snatch another few minutes of delicious solitude for the self. Even if that self was so abstracted, that it wasn't especially aware of it being a self right now. But at least it wasn't intruding that shrivelled creature, she who is her daughter's mother.

Sure enough Teagan brought her mother's idle reverie to an end as she ambled into the kitchen. Piercing the anaemic protection of the magic circle inscribed on the formica surface by a coffee ring from her mug. She braced herself by driving her weight down on the breakfast stool's upholstery. Here it comes she thought. That avowal to herself and congruent covenant with her daughter, that she would never be too busy, or distracted, or spent, to not fully and seriously address any guileless inquiry that might be launched at her. Whatever was going on in her daughter's world always out-trumped that of her own. Not that anything of significance was ever happening in her own world these days, its horizons having somewhat shrunk and sunk beneath the breakfast bar countertop level that capstoned her daughter's realm.

"Mummy?"

"Yes petal?"

"I want you to paint my bedroom a different colour."

Well she hadn't seen that one coming. She momentarily speculated whether this was linked to the serious bout of distemper from last year, when she had discovered evidence of her daughter inscribing the wallpaper with her crayons and felt-tipped pens. In Teagan's callow mind, a wall as inviting expanse of blank canvas to be imprinted upon, was merely the natural extension of sketch pad and colouring-book. This had holed the almost continuous plimsoll line of her tolerance, so she hadn't managed that admonition with her usual sang-froid moderation. Instead she had flown off the handle at her small fry, in denouncing it as vandalism. She should have steeled herself to embrace the precocious, if primitive graffiti art, that ebulliently underscored a recent mastering of brandishing a stylus with controlled strokes. No such mitigations entered her head at the time, instead she was ratcheted up to the similar state of being, as to when their house had been burgled and she'd felt personally violated. Her steaming fury was only lanced by the ingenious counter from her articling litigator, that had not she, mother that is, herself not emblazoned the paintwork of her bedroom door, by making her stand by the lintel and marking her height with a Sharpie pen on the wood? After a bout of wordless gurgling, that particular bone of contention was buried post haste. And she didn't gauge that her puppy dog of a daughter was disinterring it here and now. But blow her if she had any idea what she was alluding to. What bamboozling byzantine thread of bambino logic she was drawing on and out.

"What do you mean petal?"

"The lady on the TV said that your life is a story and you can change it by painting your walls a different colour."

Did she now? A prophetess or seer no doubt from one of those awful lifestyle programmes that pepper daytime television. For people who have no lives to do anything with except adorn them with fripperies. Or an advert perhaps? Something heavily prescripted either way. She needed to get her own script spot on here and now.

"Your bedroom doesn't need painting, love. It's got that lovely teddy bear wallpaper you like."

She scrunched her nose in contemplation. Seems her mother had offered a reasonable opening gambit. Hopefully her little 'un would fold. That her stamina was flagging before the fresh energy lift of teatime sucrose.

"Maybe just the ceiling then?"

"Well ceilings are usually always white. They need to be white to reflect the light from the lampshade to spread it over the whole room and keep it bright. So you can see to read in it." Is any of that even right? She thinks she just made it up. More blasted Physics. Who knew it was so central to motherhood?

"Well we could choose another light-coloured colour. Like yellow."

Aw, utterly delightful how she got all tangled up in her words there. "You want to be looking up at ceiling of custard every time you lie in bed?" Good one Mum. You got a laugh out of her. Keep it light. Make it all the big joke that it is. Meanwhile the lounge ceiling was verging on yellow from her husband's nicotine overlay. Maybe they could double up and have both done. How very bloody dare they peddle their wares with such a tag line!

"Alright, not yellow then. Pink!"

"Darling, you can't change your life with a change of colour scheme. It doesn't work like that." The first significant mention of pink. Is this the stage when she now falls into line with the stereotype of the little girl? Is this how she will brand herself? No, she's got more character than that. She is her own little person. Wilfully so.

"Yes, she said you could change it with deluxe? Like the pizza with four different halves each with different toppings."

"Four quarters sweetpea. And it's 'Dulux' darling. That's the name of a bra- a make of paint. Deluxe is when something is really luxurious, the best possible quality."

"Apart from special pizzas."

"Yes. Apart from pizzas."

"They should have called it 'Deluxe' then? I want 'Due-lux' for making my life deluxe."

Now she's positively playing with the putty of words!

Could have been worse, she could have caught it as 'Durex'. Could have been far worse, could have been one of their old traditional ads with a big old shaggy English Sheepdog and she'd be asking for one of those rather than a new lick of paint. She had found it funny that a decorative paint company had opted for its mascot, a dog so inbred that it was prone to the clouded vision of cataracts. "Petal, how do you think changing the colour of your bedroom would possibly change your life?" Besides there are no guarantees of a deluxe life from anything. Not even love. She wishes there were, but there ain't.

"I don't know how it works, but I want to give it a try."

"Why do you think you need to change your life anyway?" What's so bad about it that you want to cast it off like a snake sheds its skin and grow a new one? Has she failed you this terribly? In just four and a half years?

"Because I think I'm tired of teddy bears now."

"Ah okay, you want a change in your bedroom. But that's not quite the same as a change in your whole life." Infants 'tire' of things. Teens get 'bored' with them. And adults? What's left for them? Just ennui.

"It shows I'm getting older. Growing up. That's change."

"Ha true! Very true. But don't be in any rush to grow up honeybun. Enjoy your childhood, it's all about- it's so totally full of fun." No responsibilities. Nobody reliant on you. Eke out your childhood for as long as you can stave off being an adult. Though the professionals tell you that's not healthy either. Anyway, that's becoming more and more of a remote possibility. With daily solicitations importuning you to buy stuff manifestly not restricted to just adults now. The gloves are off and kids are game. A ripe new market. Pester power. Although this isn't for a toy or a game. Or clothes. This is a bit more… oblique. Still messing with her head though. And by proxy, now her own too. Wait, she spends all day with her, she doesn't have to beat herself up. She has nothing to feel guilty about Teagan being deprived of either affection or attention.

"Well it would be fun to repaint my room. We could do it together. That would totally be fun."

Damn it! She's seen right through that one. If she'd been devoting her full attention instead of beating a retreat into here, she would never have become prey to that advert in such an exposed manner. Had she have stayed present in the room, she could have easily disarmed through distraction; but once it was lodged in her daughter's imagination enough to have raised her from the sofa to seek out the oracle here in the kitchen, then it takes on a whole new heft. It's never enough is it? It can never be enough. The onslaught is perpetual. It's impossible to guard against it. Now you are enjoined never to take your eyes off them for a second. To save them from the come hithers and seductions of the marketers and advertisers. "Sweetie, if we had your bedroom repainted, we'd get a professional decorator in. He'd do far better a job than either you or me. You'd want your room to look perfect and nice afterwards wouldn't you? If I did it, it would be full of paint blobs on the wall. I'm afraid house paint is totally different to the paints and brushes you use." And which until recently, she'd wielded together alongside with her. She only stopped… Simply because she thought Teagan no longer wanted her mother to paint with her. That she'd demonstrated an independence of mind on that score.

"But if a man did it, it wouldn't be my story would it? It would be his?"

"Pardon? What story?"

"The lady in the advert said –"

"Yes I remember what you said she said –" Calm down, keep it even. Four years old and she already wants a story for herself? Why? Is the pell-mell world too inchoate for her to locate herself in it? Too fleeting to moor herself assuredly with a fixed sense of self? Hard to credit given her mainly spending her time sat down at the table colouring in or watching children's TV. The way she plays with her dolls' house seems possessed enough. Does she yearn for their stories? Is she fabricating alternative lives through them? Careful, deep breath here. Because stories help make sense of things. Arrange things into recognisable patterns. But there is pattern a plenty in her life as of now. Nursery, swimming lessons, dance class, trips to the library. The regular repeating pattern of teddy bears across her wall-paper, which she now reports to have wearied of. What story does she imagine herself to have at this tender threshold? Other than that written in the stars. The parents she's condemned to be reared by, inevitably imprinting on her story. "Darling, nobody's life is a story. You have to live your life, not write it out first. You can't make life fit perfectly to your plan. Like paint, it's lumpy and bumpy rather than smooth. It's like one of your colouring books where sometimes you shade outside the thick black border. Nobody minds that." Good job Mum, paint life as one great big anxiety. Ratchet up the unease. God almighty, keep a sense of perspective. And let her keep her dreams.

"Well if it doesn't matter if we go outside the lines, then you and I can do it ourselves can't we?"

"It doesn't matter if children go outside the lines but grown-ups can't. That's the difference between being a child and an adult." Adults have to be professional, to take pride in their work. She is now her work. Her life's work. Her profession even. Is she taking enough pride in it? Is she putting the requisite shift in? She's got to nail her soft-sell now, as a counter-narrative. Christ to be even thinking in such terms. "Teagan, your story is just starting. It can go in any direction, so there's no need to change anything. There's nothing to change just yet anyway. Go with the flow, see wherever it leads you." Oh that puckered brow again. "Look, you know in your stories how you have a beginning, middle and then the end? That's a story. It starts and it finishes. But life, real life, is all the stuff in the middle." It just goes on and on, day after day, week after week, month after month, year after year. Real enticing huh? She'll not introduce the concept of death and cessation at this juncture perhaps. "Life has no story. No pattern you can just wake up one day and change with a fresh coat of paint." Reinstate those dreams poppet. Say it enough times and maybe she'd start believing it herself. "A story in a book is fixed. No matter how many times you read it, things happen in the same way every time. But life can't be fixed and held to just one thing. And certainly not with a plan. You can be anything you want in your life. And you can change at any point in time. There's no limit. There is no end." Who can even remember their beginning as a baby? Everyone's opening chapter is just blank. A baby has no words and no memories, so that makes it a mite tough to construct any narrative. Apart from what your parents contrive to formulate for you. Did her mother fret and worry about her fragile burgeoning identity in her kitchen? Did she hell! "That lady lied to you." Fibbed, she should have said 'fibbed'!

More scrunching up of her features. Did she go too far after all? Has she killed the love of stories in books for her? Flaming advertisers!

"Okay, so I can't really change my life like that. But can we still change my teddy bear wallpaper?"

"Of course we can darling."

That flipping advertiser had communed with her daughter. Showing her how to stare right into her mother's soul.

Mummer

China dolls and Bisques with their life-like skin tones cast in porcelain. Rag dolls and Cabbage Patch Kids. Baby dolls and the ubiquitous Ken and Barbie. Dolls that cry for their feed and dolls that wet themselves enjoining your further attention. Dolls that speak if you poke their stomachs. Wooden, plastic and textiled. The unjointed and those with movable limbs. Matrioshkas and poppets. Funerary figures and fertility dolls in the psychologist's consulting room. A police doll mascot in the detective's office, like you see in those clip joints for tourists. Lugubrious fixed smile plastered across its face.

Dolls were handed down from mother to daughter in my family. The smell of dead matriarchs preserved in the darkened grain of the venerable wood. Until the heritable doll was placed in my sacred trust, when its careworn infirmity and age finally did for it and the rotted wood fell apart.

Leaving me clutching a lone arm in grotesque salute, while the head and torso lay collapsed and dismembered in a heap at my feet. The lone occasion when I had, albeit unintentionally, been able to articulate the gnarled block of hardwood that the doll had petrified into.

So what did I have to pass on to my daughter Portia, other than narrative tales of naughtiness and cheeky derring-do from my own childhood creation Polly Dolly? Portia thrilled to Polly Dolly's mischievous exploits, with fists over her mouth to rein in forbidden giggled identification with Polly's disobedience. These were tales I told her in bed, recounting the dimly remembered history of my own little girlish play. I wasn't sure if I regretted not keeping any of the plastic surrogates which replaced the entombed heirloom homunculus, to pass on to Portia or not. She didn't seem to be going short though, arrayed as they were like a guard of honour against the walls running along two sides of her bed.

I was intrigued to know if my narratives were adopted by Portia in her own play. I pried into her ventriloquistic soliloquies to see if any of Polly Dolly's sparkling Socratic dialogues seeped into the tea party, as the doll hostess patiently poured imaginary cuppas for each of her sorority who sat back floppily on their chairs. But it hadn't. She was neither repeating nor reiterating our shared world. There was no Polly Dolly in attendance. Seems I had not been able to initiate a new family lineage of my own. The irony of course is that virtually every aspect of her play mimicked what I did in real life. For what is a doll but a simulacrum of a daughter? Telescoping her into motherhood, caring for the plastic or cloth tot that was her. Well now her father has also got in on the act, scooping her up (and out) and hurling her headlong into adulthood in the worst possible way imaginable. Like her, he has confused the effigy and the real.

Anatomically accurate dolls. A new one on me. To add to the list, along with the voodoo doll which I can no longer exclude. Who even manufacturers them? What do you do for a living? Oh, I manufacture anatomically correct dolls. I sew the penises and vaginas on. You must be so proud. No, not especially. They're so ugly. The human frame is actually hideous in reality. Proper dolls are endearing. An idealised human form so you can fall in love with them. How could you possibly be attracted to an anatomically correct one? The dolls hadn't been brought out straight away. Portia had to tell them first. In her own words. Not theirs. These practitioners were carefully drilled in the rhetorical device of not leading a witness. Not to feed her anything to latch on to and run with. 'And how did that make you feel'? How do you think it made her flipping feel? The bleeding art of the open-ended obviousness. But then who am I to talk on the score of the obvious? The police were the same, keeping their words all business. This was a witness they could not lay verbal caltrops for. And finally, especially not my words. I was only allowed in the room at all, because she would not proceed in without me. I wasn't permitted to say anything, which was both an outrageous precondition and a blessed relief. I was just supposed to be this wall of vaguely comforting familiarity for her. Which begged a question, since I was coming to an utterly laggardly realisation, that I was anything but comforting. Or familiar.

For when they finally opened up the dollhouse of our nuclear family, they found Goldilocks me asleep in my bedroom with invisible blinkers and unseen earplugs, while Daddy Bear was off in Portia's room down the landing lapping up porridge. How could I not be aware? Surely I must have woken up in the middle of the night and frisked with a hand, only to hit the unoccupied sag in the mattress next to me and maybe the cold blast of empty air? How was I to know such silence signalled the bruit of a brute? I'd observed how daintily Portia always tucked in her dolls beneath the sheets of a toy bed and now my mind is racing to him using the same finesse to escape the environs of our shared bed, then to lift the flap of Portia's and presumably to delicately tuck her back in afterwards like it was all just a bad dream on her part. How else could I not detect the signs in the cold light of day? Portia's withdrawal, my husband's fidgety furtiveness around me. Was I his blow-up doll, insufficient to meet his needs? I who would, albeit through apathy and the wont of a quiet life punctuated by sonorous mummered groans and operatic screams, let him have his oats. Or so I conceived. Yet size does matter apparently. Presumably he desires a smaller fit than mine, stretched by Portia's difficult birth. Difficult and yet a complete breeze in light of the life I was actually delivering her into. Squaring the family circle. (Squiring the family infernal?) The wretched geometry of this domestic triangle. Lopsidedly scalene, with all angles miserably acute.

No wonder Portia always insisted on dressing, undressing, and bathing herself. I took it for an estimable sign of precocious independence. I had no idea it was covering up the branded stigmata of indentured submission before her father. After all, there had been the occasion when she had observed me at my vanity mirror with my eye pencil and gone rummaging among her own crayons to try and wreak the same on one of her dolls, only to be stymied by the vinyl plastic's impermeability. But in time as she was introduced to the Sharpie, she returned to her laboratory and proceeded to draw on some makeup, superficially with more success. Only the markings looked like scars. Blisters of butchered skin. Anatomically correct dolls? They bear neither the bruising, nor the torn membrane beneath flesh, so how anatomically representative can they possibly be? How could I not see it? When she was asked to consider the crate chock-full of arrayed dolls, with all the care she might in a stacked toyshop and to select two dolls that were the best fit for her and daddy. 'Fit', ugh! She took her time in line with the instructions about gender, ethnicity and maturity, although not presented to her in so many words. And when she complied with the request, the size differential becomes even more blatant for me to register. The mismatch. The no-contest. The abomination.

I had no doll to pass down to her, and now she is asked to accessorise herself as a doll by pointing to proxy areas of contact. It is too much to watch. I regret she demanded my presence here, though perhaps it is fitting penance for being so blind to what was going on under my own roof. Yet these dolls are not to become the agent of child's play (child splay more like). No, they are intended to usher her softly but precisely into the adult world. To sharpen up her words into crystal-tipped precision. To map the topography of a violated body. To determine the extent of the infraction of transgressed boundaries. A show and tell quite unlike the one for which she brought her favourite doll into school. There the stress was all on the 'tell', to encourage language skills and communication to her peers. Here she had passed through the 'tell' stage and the adults still want a whole hell of a lot more. There were no tea sets in the crate for these dolls. They were to be the personification of anti-social behaviour. With locked rictus smiles. Don't poker players have telltale 'tells' that give away their hands? My husband is a lousy card player on his lads' nights in, yet he never hinted at anything to me to give himself away. To betray signs of his betrayal. Maybe a hand of cards was just too trifling for him to concern himself with employing his dark arts of dissembling (and disassembling). Yet I can't help but wonder as those men sat round the baize table with their whisky tumblers and cigars, regaling one another of their sexual trysts and conquests, exactly what codes he spoke in to cloak his true inamorata?

Seeing as these figures were not for playing with, I wonder if this is going to ruin her love of dolls? That their meaning is forever going to be indelibly stamped with how they're used here today. No more make-believe, pretend and imagination, these dolls are to be the very opposite of all that. They are to fundamentally embody her own body. A further distancing of it from poor Portia, from that already initiated by her own father. Though the way he did it almost inevitably must have involved play and pretend and make-believe. Not least since all us others for so long were made to believe everything was normal and hunky-dory. But primarily to make Portia credit that his behaviour was anything but predatory and exploitative. Bastard. What perverse and perverted stories was he spinning her? (And how could Polly Dolly compete?) What delusory tales of domestic bliss was I spinning for myself now as an adult?

Neither doll is undressed. Just, well clothes are parted to one side. It makes me weep. She had already reported that her clothes had stayed 'on', but now her little fingers are tremulously modifying that small word of infinite insufficiency. She doesn't have the concept, after all in potty training we taught her pants down, not shoved to one side. Who toilet trained her, was it me or him? Can't even remember that now. Every stage of development seems to wipe clean all the memory banks of previous stages. Only I wasn't aware that he was forcibly ushering her several stages ahead. Where I failed to glean any memories to lose. Accelerating her into an adulthood destined to be forever frozen at this juncture of her childhood. Since assuredly neither Portia or I will ever erase these memories. This room with its jaunty paint scheme. The grating sympathetic lilt of the interviewer. The psychologist's room with her Freudian knick-knacks. The desperate functionality of the police station. These blessed dolls, the stuff of nightmare.

Or maybe rather than lacking the concept, she just doesn't have the vocabulary? No that's ridiculous, in her statement, ('her statement' how grotesque and alien does that sound?) she demonstrated a sophisticated battery of terms for parts of the body. Where would she have come by those? I would have transmitted some of them for sure, but many would never have crossed the threshold of my lips. They must have come from his dirty, calloused mouth. Words she knows by rote, but not how to use them. I think that is what the interviewers are utilising the dolls for. The emphasis seems to be on firming up what Portia explicitly means by 'under', 'over', 'top', 'bottom', 'behind', 'front', 'in' and 'on'. Prepositions. Pre-positions. Relationships of two bodies in space to one another. Their constellational orbits, when I have been fully eclipsed. Seems like the subject and predicate nouns are not in question. Of course not, how could they be? And the verbs? The verbs just make me shudder. I'm glad the dolls enact the verbs. So I don't have to see them falteringly being shaped on her quivering labia. Factuality correct dolls...

Hero Sum Total

Byron saved the day at his nursery school's nativity play. Both the infant Joseph and Mary had dried up and forgotten their lines. Not through an abortive trial of faith, rather through the ordeal of performing in public, which culminated in stage fright. But cometh the hour of a most pregnant pause, Byron had stepped forward into the breech birth, grabbing the plastic doll representing their divine delivery by the leg and waving it around in the air like a fescue, extemporising mightily to reignite the dramatic action. He annunciated his opinion that the newborn needed a nappy change, although wafting his free hand across his nose he vocally conceded it could be the poop in the stable from the horses or their own mule and by the smell, what were they feeding it, curry? Fortified by the peals of laughter from the audience, he then accosted the wise men and demanded that they hand over their gifts for god's elect son and that they had better be good presents from the toyshop and not just some useless herbs and other 'smellies' because none of that would overcome the stench of animal ordure. As the wise men agitatedly thrust their ersatz tissue-papered packages at the babe in his arms like pinball table flippers, Byron shucked them off and started tossing the doll up in the air and catching it as if a rugby ball. He proclaimed it as proof of magical divinity, since the child could 'fly'. Less than true to the original narrative and a touch lacking in the sacred, but the audience roared their approval with a standing ovation and calls for an encore. Byron had not only saved the show but stolen it. Yet he was not strutting around like a cock of the walk, since to his eye he had seen a void and merely moved to fill it. Like the story of the boy with the dike in Holland that they had heard in class. Rather than grandstanding, he took his place in the group bow, though his cardboard and tissue paper crown did not topple from his head as with his fellows when they dipped towards the horizontal. Perhaps this was a sign of his own elect nature after all. At the after-show party of diluted cranberry juice and crisps, adults came up and shook his hand or tousled his hair through the crown's fontanelles and heralded him a total star.

Byron was the first to admit he was not the best rugby player in his school. It was a sport where certain physical dimensions absolutely determined your position on the field and he was not particularly blessed to be so appointed. He was not tall, chunky, fleet of foot, whippy of wrist, nor with a low centre of gravity. He was, well, just somewhere in the middle. Maybe that's why he had been stationed in a position called 'centre'. Or 'centre-three-quarter' to give it full fractional due. And right at this moment, with both the game and the schools' championship title on the line, he found himself the last line of defence as the opposition wing three-quarter bore down on him. It was just the two of them within range of one another, the rest having been left floundering in their wake. The opponent was quicker than Byron, so if he got past him, there was no way of catching him back up and preventing him crossing the try line for the winning score. Byron had to stand tall, difficult when his opponent had several inches and pounds on him, more so when the technique of the rugby tackle demanded a low crouch in order to wrap your hands around the ball carrier's legs. The trouble with such a stance, was that it telegraphed your intention and made it easier for the runner to swerve or scissor into a change of direction that would leave you very much flat-footed. So Byron did stand up tall, let the juggernaut come on to him and run him over, but then clamped his arms around the boy's muscular thighs as he was trod underneath like some roadkill. More rodeo than knight's tourney, nevertheless it was his adversary who was unsaddled through Byron's desperate bear-hug. In doing so he lost his grip on the ball, which spewed forward in contravention of the sideways or backwards only motion rule, entailing the referee whistling for the infringement and turnover of possession. His team mates punched the air at the same time as the tackled player finally hit the ground, one of his metal studs catching Byron in the jaw and making him involuntarily bite the inside of his cheek.

Byron knew that his team mates were reacting only with jubilation, but their delirious slaps on his back and bear-hugs of their own, sent searing jolts of pain through his bloodied mouth. They declared him a leg-end before hoisting him on their shoulders and marching him off the field like some ancient conquering hero. Their unsteady, unregimented formation, odd given how much they drilled in training on the Roman tortoise of a scrum and the ballista that was the line-out, perfectly syncopated his own swaying, as he veered towards fainting with the pain and the sight of blood staining his jersey. But he was determined not to fall and made it to the changing rooms. His mouth was seen to by the school nurse while the head coach addressed all the boys in their triumph. Byron was singled out for praise for the first time amongst his superior team mates, as the coach's peroration climaxed with the exhortation that there were those with the skills to win games and then there were those warriors with hearts of lions who could prevent games being lost, like Byron there, bloodied but unbowed. He then wound up with an admonition not to fritter their energies over the holidays with girls, beer and general delinquency as some sort of misguided precocious proof of manhood. Only the trial of combat out there on the field could properly confer that. Byron might have been nodding in accord, or perhaps it was more of a wince, as the first aid needle went through the inside of his cheek to apply the lead off in a line of stitches.

Byron's reflexes were sharp. He was walking behind an old lady when a lick of wind whisked the wide-brimmed straw hat from her pate and sent it cartwheeling down the road. Byron flew off from the pavement to pinion it. Cars honked reproach for his seeming recklessness, chorused with bellowed inquiries as to whether he had a death-wish. The lady clasped her wizened hands together and placed the tips of her fingers over the small gape of her mouth, though Byron couldn't be certain if this gesture of apprehension was for him or her hat. He thrust out the floral millinery in front of him self-evidently, but the very incongruity only seemed to inflame the drivers' ire more, as in their windscreens they shook their fists at this crazed kid with his flimsy superhero's shield. He returned towards her, gently brushing the dust and grit from the soft crown, at which point the motorists revoked their vexation and melted into smiles. Byron gently held the brim by the pads of his fingers before re-anointing it upon her quivering head. The cars moved off with a symphony of approbatory honking in an impromptu trumpet voluntary. She proclaimed him "My hero" as she grasped his wrist with her twig-like fingers.

"Oh I don't know about that" he replied, "anyone would have done the same."

She patted his wrist, "No, I'm not sure they would. Not these days. But let's not dwell on that, such an act of chivalry deserves a reward."

She fished from her pocket a wrapperless sweetie swaddled between crumpled and possibly used tissues. Byron couldn't help but dry swallow. The sweet looked most unappetising. She pressed it into his palm and then closed his fingers back over it. He was grateful that at least the confection wasn't sticky against his flesh. Now came the true test of his bravery, not that mere tourneying with steel chassised steeds. Could he bear to bring himself to slip the amorphous bonbon into his mouth? Less jawbreaker, more germ warfare. He took the plunge and popped it in. He didn't even close his eyes and managed an obliging smile, though he did feel sick to his stomach. Whether by thought or by actual unsavouriness he could not separate out.

Byron was at the ephebe's crossroads. That final part of the academy's training him for citizenship. In addition to his choice of A-Level subjects with an eye to the specialisation at university, was the weighty choice of extracurricular activities. Since he was being asked to opt for either the cadet corps, or social welfare volunteering. He attended introductory appetisers for both. At the cadet corps' open day, he was among his old rugby comrades which he thought slightly curious, since they had to a man (boy?) comprehensively failed to heed their coach's admonition and spent the summer dissipating their energies and diluting their commitment, instead reorienting their dedication to the girls' school abreast of their own. One thing Byron knew about the military was that it demanded discipline and regimentation. But beyond that, he wondered if it would offer any new experiences beyond the rigours of training and teamwork he had already notched through sport. On the other hand, he didn't know the kids he found himself witnessing the social welfare presentations with. His own ad hoc acts of social kindness had all been individual, so he found it hard to conceive how social welfare could be executed in groups. The samplers and tasters for the soup kitchen, the old people's home, or reading to the blind, showed him that indeed there would be only two students assigned to each duty. So that ushered in his first dilemma, to reconvene being part of a troop, or in the main to fly solo. Synergism versus individual relationship. Offering two different sources and perhaps scales, of esprit de corps.

Byron was stymied over which path to take. He sought the advice of his parents.

"No son of mine is going off to any army," stammered his mother in disbelief, her hands slamming into the sink's water and depth-charging a cataract of displaced suds.

"It's hardly an army, more playing at it," retorted his father.

"Toy soldiers? That's even worse," she impugned, wheeling round on him, gesticulating in his direction with

Marigold gloves and soapy lather tattooing her upper arms.

"Why? It will do him a world of good, provide a sense of adventure and make a man of him," his father endorsed. They continued to squabble back and forth much to Byron's dismay. His father pointed out that both Byron's grandfathers had seen active duty, so that there was not an insignificant proud family tradition of it. His mother folded her arms scathingly and cross-pollinated the soap suds to pearl necklace herself, as she counterpointed that was completely irrelevant to determining his destiny, since it had hardly been passed down the bloodline given that he was a chartered accountant and she a librarian. His father conceded that point, but blustered that both men had leapt to the defence of their nation and proved to be heroes. His mother became apoplectic at this contention, tearing off her Marigolds and exploding that a true hero was he or she who managed to raise a healthy and properly turned-out family, to provide food and clothing for them, rather than he who wanted to detonate the chances for others in different parts of the world to do the same. Why always this preternatural drive to rise above the rest of humanity and conquer to stoop? A hero could only ever have their pretensions burst, to experience a crushing defeat, or at least a massive non-fulfilment of such a grandiose self-image. Greek Tragedy showed us that in spades, as she threw the rubber gloves on to the draining board. His father snickered at her passion, mockingly conferred upon her the title of hero, or heroine, at the centre of her own little monodrama being played out here in the kitchen. The boy was only going to indulge in some square-bashing, so this was hardly cause for "The Trojan Women"; he just prayed the consequence of this little bone of contention wouldn't result in any

"Lysistrata" sanctions.

Before his wife could quench her fume sufficiently to recover her voice, he went on to prognosticate that the problem here, was Byron being patently unable to show decisiveness, to take control over a very minor aspect of his life and choose an activity, that in the great scheme of things amounted to very little. And thereby was the conundrum in a nutshell, the vision of life she offered up for Byron here on his very threshold of entry, was one of utter mediocrity. You had to set yourself some, a few, ambitious targets to try and make something of this one-shot deal that was life. To attempt to leave your mark on the world, whether it be setting some sporting record, or contributing some permanent body of work to the human pool of knowledge, or even as Byron had discovered so precociously, to just entertain a crowd of people and give them a right royally good time. Besides, what with all the humanitarian work the military does these days, there was very little difference between the army and social work. Was social work not just the home version of the very benighted souls she had fostered in her argument about civilians displaced by war? Far better however, not to be pre-destined as one of those unfortunates requiring assistance, but to forge on ahead robustly and with the confidence to look the world in the eye instead of cowering from it. Kill the natives, then issue them a sticking plaster she blustered. She scoffed that she was surprised that a demigod such as he, King of the Risk Averse and Prince of the Derivative, deigned to dwell among mere mortals in such a humble home. Oh, so she didn't respect his job now was that the thing, he charged? Here's some numbers for you, zero multiplied by anything is still zero. And any number divided by zero is infinity she shot back at him.

Actually it's not, it's indefinable, but who's counting?

Look, he didn't want to clip his son's wings through any lack of spirit and avidity, even if his own flames had been a tad doused. She rounded on him, demanding to know if he ascribed her the cause of such wet blanketing of his ambitions? Before he could answer she spewed a litany of accusations against him, each one syncopated with her smashing a plate on the floor in front of him. How there was nothing mutually funded about their marriage since she had brought to it a sizeable dowry. That he was all about accruals and depreciation and not in a finance sense of the terms. He was chief hedger and CEO of a non-ongoing concern, from the school of if it ain't broke, make it broker. He had used up all her goodwill, his promissory notes had long expired their redemption dates and seeing as he had no more credit in the marriage, this particular partnership should be considered for wind-up and dissolution. Did he know of any good receivers? Parent company, ha that was a misnomer, for he didn't keep her company at all in the upbringing of their son, so there was nothing equitable about their responsibilities, she being the only one in this family who undertook due diligence for Byron's fate and over her dead body would he become collateral damage for the British Army and government. There was nothing at all heroic about coming back from a distant land in a body bag, because you'd stepped on a land mine disguised as a yak turd, or someone had blown you up with a signal from their cellphone, yet that was exactly how the authorities would spin it, as she ran her foot over the smashed shards of crockery and made them crackle. What with the stately unloading of the coffin from the airplane, wrapped in a Union Jack and trumpeted along its lugubrious pace shouldered by six men in formal army uniform, not fatigues note, but formal dress. Is that truly what he wanted for their son? His father was bursting with a girandole of rebuttals, but as he too deliberately ground the crockery back and forth beneath his leather shoes, he managed to select the first rejoinder, about how he found it interesting that she felt the need to legislate for Byron's 'fate'. How about vouchsafing him the freedom to make his own choices?

"Knock it off both of you" screamed Byron. The family, where both war and social work seemed ineluctably conjoined. Maybe he should just leave school now and avoid the heinous choice he was confronted with, but then no doubt it would be replicated pretty much everywhere in his search for any job as necessitated by a decision to quit education. The truly heroic act of the present age? To avoid sinking into despair. Thereby he adjudged he was destined never to be a hero.

Shelf-Help

One single word Jonah, that's all I ask. I'm desp- I want, to hear your side of the story. How you see things and view the world. I really don't have the first inkling. Why would you clam up like this all the time? It makes no sense to me. Do you expect me to be a mind reader?

I'm biting my tongue, so much so until it bleeds. Because I'm committed to providing you this receptive space to talk. Where I won't jump in all over what you say. But you've turned it into a siege. Your clenched silence has reduced me to the role of interrogator. No that can't be right, since I'm not permitted to raise questions. Overseer then. This is like the most desultory of garden tennis, or Swingball games played between you and I in the dim and distant past. When I, yet again, pared myself down and stopped up all my shots. Confined myself to your shrunken level, so as to try and engender some sort of slewed parity. I used to play tennis for my county you know? I've probably got some old photos to prove it. Would you like me to show you them? Thought as much.

I have to do something. For this simply isn't working. This let it be, has shut us both down. Prostrated us both. For all my care not to strike the wrong note, I actually think right now I'm failing to transmit on any wavelength. So, what am I going to do?

When did our communication lapse? How did I let that happen? I used to talk to you in my womb. Made up stories. Sang songs to you. I didn't have to read any self-help and how-to guides for that. Even played you some of my opera box sets. Simultaneously soothing and soaring. What a start in life I imagined that to be imbuing you for. But here in your perennial mute silence, you have repudiated me in that love affair, as well as the rest. The first note of an aria and I can see your hackles rise. I'm too apprehensive to play my music when you're at home. If either male of the house is in residence for that matter. No need to drive another wedge between us, not that you'd show me any such reciprocal consideration. I don't know, somehow I expected all that passion, all that full-lunged ardour, to cross the membrane that separated us and seep into you. But seems like it's had the opposite effect. Liebestod. Oh god!

I get that this is an assertion of self. Your liberation. That you are no longer my captive audience. But now you have gone to the other extreme. You want to enlist for maturity? To play with the grown-ups? On equal terms? Okay then, first just ask yourself what do we adults resort to for our entertainment? Why, words of course. Talking. Conversation. Gossip. The meter of our humdrum souls. The currency of commonality. We might garnish it over food, or especially drink. We may even wreathe it around films, TV shows, or newspapers and magazines. But all are mere scaffolding, stage flats with mounted backdrops, for us collecting together to dialogue. To bandy words. Arming yourself with stories about others, to parry their stories about you. Or we become the centre of our own stories. If we can't land a grudging compliment, then maintaining an even keel, we do others down so we look better by comparison. A sliding scale of approbation and degradation. We're witty and catty, we goad and we coax... But only in the company of other grown-ups. Where provoking exasperated silences are rated minor triumphs. You've got that part down pat at least.

Believe me, you don't want to be in any great rush to plunge headlong into that. See, it's all change yet again to ascend to the next level. You know, like on one of your video games? Since it's an intricate balance to strike. You don't want to cause anyone true harm with what emerges from your mouth. Adults at play, we have to gauge it to josh right. It all has to be done with affection. We dote through our personal anecdotes. Our privileged audience of friends to whom we chose to reveal ourselves. It takes time to assimilate that scale, usually learned through the experimentation of teenagehood. Where hormonal mouth and brain scarcely talk to one another. Scant proofreading before reacting to some parental edict or other. All those wounding things adolescents fling at their parents. Yet seemingly not you. Only it's glaringly transparent to me, that the tiny motion of you drawing in your bottom lip there, is you essaying to suck back your words. To blot them all up and stave off any escaping across the labial threshold into auditory range. It just occurs to me the irony of the term 'expressing milk' as squeezing out for another to imbibe – which I palpably failed to do for you – and here now is your own failure to express yourself clearly and unambiguously to me in turn. See even though no exchange has passed between us, I have unearthed a link. A link, though not necessarily a root cause. What I can't pierce, is whether you stifling your own speech is an act of denying me and my insinuating pull on you, or because you are protecting me from your seething ire.

I won't deny the adult social reflex is largely to fill the empty air, recently vacated by someone else's fleeting vacuity, with some evanescent puff of your own. It matters not what shape this air is sculpted into, merely that it is given body. Words as landfill, or in this case, airfill. And it's maybe a good thing that you're rising above all that puff. But as your mother, I'm still offering you a special communion. Brimful with meaning. Our own unique discourse. An exclusive language belonging solely to the two of us. What do you say? Our aegis against the world. I don't expect our full reincorporation, so why should you? Nothing. Not a flicker. I'm fooling myself. You've gone all foetal wholly outside my body.

Of course I may have this entirely wrong. Being a bit behind the times and all that. It wouldn't be the first instance. From what I read nowadays, the available technology has changed the world for you kids. How the teenage years are no longer just a gestation period for you. Armed to the budding wisdom teeth with all the linguistic tools just going mouldy on the branch, never afforded an opportunity to unleash the overripe, bitter, bilious fruit of despair. No, now you are already furnished with the means for immediate emotional redress. Minute-flat digital catharsis. For doubtless there is already an innumerable cache of words, not just bottled, but actually brewed fresh in your crucible. Primed for when I depart, to be decanted behind my back and instantaneously served up to your intimates on the internet. Virtual matricide in group chatrooms and a Flickring dagger to the heart, enabling others to Stumble Upon my corpse. I can only hope that you also air some opinions on the world in general, as seen from your own blossoming outlook. Please don't let it be just a constant tirade, bad mouthing all and sundry closest to you. I couldn't bear to think that was your primary address to the world. That solely which was driving you to express yourself. To resort finally to words.

Okay, I have regathered myself. I realise it rests on my shoulders to break our impasse. To make the next move. So I need to do something unexpected, something out of the ordinary, in order to wrench your attention. An act to acknowledge my actuality. And to trip yours. A grand gesture, or maybe a subversive one, rather than mere wordfill. I could ring you on your mobile. Wistfully admire the reflex with which you scrabble to consult it, anticipating some friend on the other end. In full contrast to me being poised just ten foot away from you. Passing me over with alacrity. Flouting your erasure of me. Rubbing it in my voided face. The problem is I'd have to leave the room to go and retrieve my phone and make the call from beyond here. That would doubtless tip you the wink. Besides, even if it didn't, you're sure to recognise my number in caller ID and refrain from reacting. I suppose that's rather presuming you have my number still listed in your contacts. Unless maybe I opt for performing it as a deliberate act, so I'm wafting it right in your face. Paging my son to talk to his Mum. The only way to get through to you, being down some fibre optics sat under the ocean, bouncing signals off a distant mast. Even you would have to infer that as a farcical way to relate.

I swear I'm going to make a pyre of all those completely useless self-help books. Right here in your room, right under your nose. That would get you up and shifted. Wait a minute, what about tidying your room around you? Bring a bit of bustle to this standstill. Set the vacuum to blow rather than suck, see if that way we can inject some agitation into the settled dander in here. Ruffle the duck down under your head. Drive you from your perpetual layover and thrust us both in a new direction. The noise alone ought to be enough, though for good measure I could always thwack it a few times against your bedstead, as I accidentally on purpose misjudge the height clearance. Conceivably I suppose I might not be able to hear you above the din, were you finally to pipe up. That split-second window when I can see your lips moving, but fumble away valuable moments trying to silence the mechanical salvo. And in that moment, my racket is tumbled and you choke me off once again.

So, okay now, let's consider all the ramifications. What's a quick swish around with the vacuum actually going to achieve? Might be better off taking down your curtains and popping them in the washing machine. Expose you to view. Remove a layer of cocooning wrap. That would engender more of a significant reverberation. A rayon gauntlet thrown down. It might be all very well you staring into nothing, a glassy eyed angel with features shrouded not by a halo but a hoodie, yet do I really want to come on the harridan with feather duster, furniture polish and face flannel? What's the best I could hope for, that you might critique my technique? Point out a spot I'd missed. Practitioner to practitioner. Houseboy to char. Incendiary to wet blanket. Mrs Mop and Master Mope. But that would suit fine. That would represent a defrosting. A jokey collusion. A gentle swapping of capacities. An acknowledgement of our former roles, to be sloughed like moults. Handing over of the torch. A tacit redrawing of new responsibilities and new status. An operetta in place of full-throated opera. I could live with that. Can you?

Secondary Picketing

The boy stood on the burning deck
Picking his nose like mad
He rolled them up into little balls
And flicked them at his dad.

Why was the boy idling, with the wooden planks from under about to ignite and consume him? Sure the smoke and ashes may have assailed his nasal passages, causing some pillaging of the mucosa, yet why at that particular critical moment was rhinotillexomania more pressing than the wellbeing of the whole body? Additionally there is the presence of his father to consider, presumably trying to whisk away his progeny into a life-boat and save him from the conflagration? Or so one would hope and yet all he received in return from his death-wishing snot, was a volleying broadside of dried mucus. None of it makes any sense.

That's disgusting, stop it at once.

A difficult gambit for success this one. Timing is the key. The notion of something being 'disgusting' assumes a moral judgement. An ever fickle sweep, from the impolitic, through the impolite, all the way up to the full-blown scandalous. Then there is the difference between an injunction against something abstract being morally wrong and that which the child can demonstrably reason for himself as being wrong. Yet, too young and the child has not developed such a sensitivity, being unable to plot a moral compass from the very large, such as the prohibition on murder, to this relatively small injunction against localised finger up the nostril. Then there is the further phase to take into account, when the 'disgusting' is actually sacred to a child. An express revelling in the unpleasant, the proscribed, the frowned upon. Green mucus is venerated in play, through tubs of ersatz green 'goo'. The word 'bogey' is delighted in and hurled around as if a powerful incantatory word. And finally, if the contention is about exhibiting it in public, does that render it acceptable if performed in the privacy of one's own room, away from prying ears?

Send me a postcard when you reach the top.

But I don't have pen and paper, I suppose I could write it in mucu-. Oh, I see what you did there mum. Very clever. I was at a loss for any comeback. But it's a one-shot stratagem. Once you scaled the summit, there's nothing more but to come back down. And so we catechised. It became our cosy routine, our fence and parry. I would still thrust up the mucal slopes, driving my cuticular pickaxe into the green rock face. While she would counter with this chastisement now stripped of all its admonitory power through repetition. I played stooge to her unfunny man. Or perhaps it was vice versa.

It will get stuck up there and you'll have to walk around with your finger up your hooter.

Stuck... hmmmm... yes. Isn't it supposedly a sign of being in the know when you tap your finger against your nose? But that's on the outside of course. Being on the inside of some secret knowledge, is symbolised by a gesture against the outside integument. Curious. Naturally no finger would ever become rooted there, since the impress of upward force has a concomitant reaction from the tissue and cartilage. The tissue expands and the cartilage flattens so as to accommodate the alien appendages. Similar to how snakes consume prey greater than their girth. However, on a couple of occasions this warning did actually caption a brace of adjustments on my part at different times. The first was that I adopted the nose-picking technique of using my little finger, in the misguided belief that it was smaller and of less intrusion upon the fabric of my nose. Some people omit their little finger from threading a teacup handle and just extend it out into the air (like a wind sock, testing for perturbations of cooling air?) My pinkie is not so redundantly effete, but rather is the mining borer ploughing ahead in the unceasing search for mineral wealth. The second adjustment, well that was when I was at secondary school and certain of my peers scanned my enlarged proboscis and muttered the word 'Jew' at me. That caused a hiatus in my ore drilling for a while, as I pondered and wrestled with the implications and associations of their single word censure. But I wasn't stilled for long. As soon as I finished school, I was back to the ceaseless prospecting. For what exactly? Castles in the air built on mucal sand.

Is your brain itchy?

How very prescient of you father, though neither of us could really see it at the time. And let's face it, the Nasal face of the KillymanGiro, Killyjoymanrow or whatever, was never going to be a propitious way to lance the boil of my fretful mind. The frontal assault not a terribly efficacious manner for reaching the Urals of grey matter deeply recessed to the east. A retreat from frigid Moscow as my brain still chafes. Chock-full of persecutory thoughts, anxieties, neuroses. All coated and smeared in words. I can always tell when such a mood is about to swoop down on me. The smell inside my nose alters. A scented harbinger of my imminent descent. Normally like most ordinary folk, I cannot smell myself through immunity rendered by long exposure. But on the precipice of an event, I get this strange sense of tasting myself, caustic and unpleasant in my nostrils. Without having any longer to insert a moistened digit to taste the wind. The prevailing direction is clear. My whole childhood was a process of seasoning me to my own tang, so that I would be able to detect deviations. The wind sock billowing in a forbidding direction. Warning of an imminent tempest.

You'll burst a blood vessel and cause a nose bleed.

Cause and effect… Yeah, there are other ways to bring about the same outcome. Such as snorting cocaine on a consistent basis. An inversion of black grit employed to forestall banks of white snow, here with white powder envisioned to disperse the black cloud looming in my head and have me expelling dark clots of dried blood. It brought short-term relief, like when you have a good hearty blow of the nose in the midst of a heavy cold. The trouble with coke is that it engenders an all-year-round ague and plays merry hell with your sinuses too. There's no shifting the discharge then. All those solid flesh and bone probes up the nostrils as a kid and never once did I bring about your premonitory fear of striking plasmatic paydirt. But the granular gossamer powder that blows away on the faintest gust of wind (hence the need for early warning windsock dispositions), does wreak terrible havoc on the capillaries and arteries. I finally scaled the muzzled apex, only by hitting rock bottom. Snuffed.

Plié Plea

Mother, remind her again why she comes to these classes? Oh yes, to get her out of the house and off her phone. To make new friends, in the flesh. To develop grace and posture and confidence in her body. Further refined by the gloss provided by her teacher; that her body must become a means of expression, to tell the story of the ballet through her movements. To personify the spirit of dance.

In essence, the girls were too young for them to be dubbed auditions, but indubitably that's what they were. And she was never selected, either in the coryphée or for a duet. Or perish the thought, for a solo. As Stella put her coat on over her ballerina's costume to begin the trudge home from another fruitless showcase, she flattened out the tutu down against her thighs, making the bottom of the coat billow out like it was containing some sort of distending flesh beneath its fabric. The other girls snickered and sneered and muttered "thunder-thighs" under their breath and Stella knew they looked down on her for her modest roots. Her costume didn't match those bespoke shop-bought ones sported by all the other nymphs, being more peach than pink. Her mother had fashioned it for her from an old bridesmaid's dress, she herself had worn in those days when she too yearned to be picked. So, no, Stella hadn't made any friends (even if she had, she wouldn't dare feel she could invite them back to her scrubby little house). And since the girls snapped surreptitious pictures of Stella on their phones and sent them to friends, or uploaded them to social media cabal and covens unknown, ballet didn't seem to be curing them of *their* phone addiction now did it?

She'd attended the performances, sat in the audience with the other students who hadn't made the cut, just to try and elicit why those on stage had been chosen and she hadn't. But for the life of her she couldn't fathom it. Their bodies didn't seem to be expressing much in the way of emotion, rather concentrating solely on executing the choreography correctly as they'd been coached. Nor were their twirling forms seemingly evoking the spirit of the dance any more than hers ever did. She glanced over to their teacher and regarded her carried away by something she saw on stage. Following her line of sight, she saw the principal dancer land a competent petit assemblé and then seemingly so pleased with herself, that she cracked open a smile to reveal a gob full of metalwork. "Bravo!" yelled the teacher and stood to start clapping loudly, and rather inelegantly, Stella thought. She just didn't get it. How was stupid ballet telling any kind of story? There were no words were there?

On the plod home she barely raised the soles of her ballet shoes from the pavement. A far cry from the swoops and whisks she had so recently performed at the barre. But then she was stopped dead in her tracks by a sight on a front lawn…

She ran rather than skipped into the house. She tugged at her mother's apron as she stood over the sink lathering dishes. "Mum, can we go visit the zoo?"

"Sure, I think I'm free this weekend."

"No now. It has to be now? Can't you leave the dishes?"

"Well okay, I guess… But don't you want to go change out of your ballet things?"

Stella shook her head vigorously and started to tug at the apron strings to encourage her mother to prepare her own array.

Her mother paid the entrance fee, silently crossing off some other activities while she balanced the household budget in her mind. As she put the derisory change back in her purse, her daughter was already studying the map laying out the animal displays around the park. The well-trodden earth at the foot of the map had turned to dust and already her mother was seething at the folly of Stella standing there in the delicate peach fabric of ballet shoes. "Shall we start with the monkey house? They're always entertaining?"

Her daughter grabbed her hand and marched them both off determinedly. "Where are we going?" but she received no reply from the firm set of her daughter's countenance. They swung away from the monkeys and snaked beyond the reptile house. They lumbered a course shy of the rhinos and elephants and loped to one side of the big cat enclosure stationed behind the fiercest of metal bars. They waddled past the sea lion and penguin pool, leaving them basking on their rock diving platforms.

They were finally stopped in front of the pond with a variety of wading birds. Her daughter dropped her mother's hand and gripped the railing with both of hers like a prison inmate. She pressed one of her cheeks through the palings which distorted her features in a most disconcerting manner.

Her mother was about to pull her back, when her hand was stayed, as her daughter raised one foot off the ground and bent it to abut her knee. She released one hand from the railing and brought it up straight, pointing towards the sky above her head. She recalled the position from her own stunted ballet days. Her daughter was executing a passé relevé, using the horizontal railing as an impromptu barre.

Then it struck her, she was echoing the stance of the flamingos on one leg with their gracefully curved necks. And surprisingly their colour was none too divergent from that of her daughter's peach tutu. She had always assumed flamingos were a shocking shade of pink. Ballerina pink. The stupid plastic ones in the neighbour's front garden certainly were. But not these specimens. She espied a keeper and asked him why their colour was not the expected vivid hue. He explained that it was due to them being in captivity, that there was no way to replicate their natural diet with its high levels of carotene that ordinarily coloured their plumage. Stella's mother didn't notice her daughter dip her head on the word 'captivity'. The choreographed posture of the body could relate a tale after all.

Skalded Like a Cat

Libraries brew their own particular smells. Not a cocktail as such, more that each section has its own distinct olfactory reference which readily classifies it. Science fiction does not smell the same as biography for example. Pick out a book from the shelf, open it up and inhale the faint spoors of all the people who have ranged across its pages. The bouquets transferred from home, where they may have read while drinking coffee, eating dinner, or curled up in bed transferring odours of soap, skin balms, or cosmetics removers. More immediately, the whiff of homeless street people, who come in for temporary shelter over at the section housing daily newspapers and periodicals. Or here in the children's section, the redolence of sour milk, sanitising nappy perfumes and for some reason, the smell of fresh baking. More rusk than Madeleine cake, for which he couldn't conceive of ever evoking any intricate literary lattice of memory.

That it should have come to this. The last vestige of the communal storytelling tradition. Him sat on a low plastic kiddie chair (or beanbag in the main branch), reading from books whose pages were dominated by line drawings, to a gaggle of toddlers clamped in place on the laps of their mothers, child minders or au pairs. Thumb-sucking their way through the oral tradition. Not much in the way of call and response, scant audience participation altogether. *Tots Tales* and *Crawler Stories* is all that remains of the proud bardic relayers of epic sagas. Of chroniclers around the camp fire bestowing the lore and history of the tribe, in order to preserve and transmit it down the generations.

He caught the librarian's signal out of the corner of his eye. Showtime. He picked up his selection of three books for today's recitation and walked over to a stack, proceeding to slide them on to a shelf at his eye level, but one towering over that of the infants. The imminent ritual of removing the books was dual-purposed. Its ceremonious nature signalled to the kids that something transformative and magical was about to transpire, through the instrumentality of the power of the book. Like Excalibur plucked from the stone. The genie sprung from the bottle. The Christ risen from his tomb. Hyperbole? Hey they're all stories from books right? Archetyped on to tree boles. While, from the library's perspective, the on-message was that such spellbinding engagement could only be uniquely obtained from the spines ranged across their very own shelves. Nonetheless he thought to himself, how it was a most odd mechanism whereby the State funded the local authority, to pay him to imbue interest and brand loyalty in the borough's free lending service. It seemed a rather indirect apparatus for promoting literacy, but there you go, he was hardly going to complain now was he? As a taxpayer, he was quite content with this use of public funds. Mind you, the books which he had just slipped into the shelves were provided from his own collection. The library couldn't be trusted to hold the titles he relied on. The system of channeling funds was not an efficient one. The magic the library purported to offer was thimblerigged.

As he hovered in place by the shelves, the librarian rose from her desk to start to round up his reluctant congregation. He noted that she possessed neither pince-nez, nor half-moon spectacles on any chain abutting her unbuttoned-up décolletage. No tight bun restrained her hair, nor was her tone stentorian towards the wayward kids. (The library, a place of words where the oral was entirely frowned upon, had now become the locus for fostering raucous verbal exchange and first expressions). How things had changed over the years. She was younger than most of the mothers in attendance and had slits in her jeans. In what manner was that going to instil any reverence for the printed word? As usual it would fall on him to salvage and repair. He would have to cast his customary spell over this flock. She sported a smile as she mock wrangled the children with pantomiming arms, since she was not allowed to actually touch them according to local by-law and code of practice. Oh for goodness sakes, if the kid doesn't want to leave off playing with the wooden train set there, then just leave him be! He could cope with a bit of background high-pitched locomotive noise. If he closed his eyes, he could imagine the 'woo-woos' to be appreciative cheering for his rendition. Closing one's eyes was hardly inimical to reading texts learned by, though not necessarily committed to heart, through countless repetitions. First time he'd 'gigged' this branch, he'd idly brushed his fingers on that train set. He couldn't believe how sticky it had been. Like glue. Or ectoplasm.

See that was the problem with modern day libraries. They were no longer exclusively shrines to the book. Instead they had kids' areas which meant greasing the wheels with a honeypot of delights other than reading material. It was the same in the adult section, with pamphlets and the internet and local government fact sheets, to distract from the paucity of actual tomes out on the shelves. Ah he hears the amateur nannying gainsayers cry, gaps on shelves translate to a stack of books being out on loan which is a good thing. Except, once a week he visited this branch, as with every branch in the borough. And each week he saw the gouges remain in the same place, never plugged up by a returned volume. At best one might postulate that they'd been stolen, in which case at least still they were being read, albeit not in the spirit of public sharing as embodied in the concept of a lending library. But it's not down to any such slow erosion through pilfering. He has witnessed piles of works removed as being obsolescent and advertising themselves on sale for the price less than an overdue fine. Some more crazy local government economics in action. But of course, the wringing hand-holders would opine, there is inevitable natural winnowing and selection. The evidence being in the date-stamped sticker of record on the inside cover. A blank sheet there is testament that the book is ripe for culling. Again, he might cede them their point, only there is never a shred of evidence of any replenishment on the shelves in their stead. What he confronts there just out of his eye line, is the bibliotheca's equivalent of a brain scan showing the gouges in the grey matter made by the assault of Alzheimer's. And like that terrible condition, soon there will be too uncritical a mass of literature here to be able to preserve any collective shared memory. He begins to have doubts, that his metaphor feels on the point of collapse. This is why he's not a writer, only a humble narrator.

He did try and write a book once. For a callow audience just such as these. But success is contingent on the illustrations and since he couldn't himself draw even a convincing stickman, he was forced to reach out and collaborate with any have-crayons-will-travel Tom, Dick or Sally. The first artiste hung on jealously to her output in response to his brief, stating that art could not be hurried. He exhorted her with a deadline by which the publisher might lose interest in the original proposal, whereupon she flounced away altogether in a huff of creative depression and took her drawings away never to be seen again, or for a first time even. The next hack took six months to misunderstand the brief and produce completely untenable and unrelated sketches to his text. The third dauber produced rather a decent fist of it but demanded too much money to part with his creations. Apparently the fantasist had visualised being able to meet this one commission then go off to retire from work altogether. The fourth and last limner produced a charming set of tableaus which so entranced the publisher, that they wanted to make her an in-house staff designer, at which point they ditched the book for good. He had protested the shabbiness of his treatment, to which the publisher just shrugged, whereupon he had raised his argument to decry the role of the children's illustrator, pointing out that without the words and the story concept, the draughtsman was left twiddling their unvarnished fingers. The commissioning editor countered with the wildly differentiating number of man hours, (or pointedly woman in this particular case), required for drafting and redrafting twelve intricate drawings and then colouring them, as against writing twenty-four lines of text distending across twelve pages. She pursed her brow as she enumerated on her fingers, the likely hours committed to devising the project; two for concretising the idea, a further two for composing the words in their entirety, another for fine-tuning, a spot of lunch down the pub, then after a nap, a quick thirty minutes for conceiving the layout and bob's your uncle, pour a celebratory glass of wine and take out a cigarette from the fag packet on which he'd likely first scribbled his brainchild. Cow was nigh bang-on. He had tried one final gambit. Elevated his dialectic to the highest point of rhetorical argument. The role of the illustrator was no different to that of the modern day conceptual artist; to wit, how their impenetrable nonsense yielded no meaning until the captioning title and/or an explanatory text, was appended to the work on display. He won the intellectual exchange but not any contract. But he wasn't bitter. He couldn't be, else he wouldn't still be in this environment, happily surrounding himself, nay immersed, in the world of ISBNs.

Moreover it does have its supplementary compensations. He can stare in through the window of the sweetie shop and feast himself gluttonously stupid in his mind. After all, he'd been doing this job for fifteen years now. Happens there's only about twelve or so decent titles worth reading and at two or three a session, he can't rotate to space them out all that much. Therefore he is able do this job standing on his head. Blindfolded even. Only he can't, see. He has to put on a display, entertain the little cherubs. Pull a few funny, non-threatening faces in the right places. Mug a visual punctuation, gurn some grammar like a good 'un. Make a big performance of turning over a page so that he underlines its narrative significance. Planting some seeds about the sequential nature of events and time, even as the little darlings are still grappling to master the persistence of objects beyond their direct observation. And, where the two come together of course, in naming and classing things, what are known in the trade as 'nouns'. Thus he looks out in the direction of his audience when he narrates. Each a proper noun in their own right, only they don't know it yet. Projects it out to them by facial expression as well as voice. But again, they're a bit too young to get much of what he's saying. So he's not really looking at the kids at all. He's taking in the mothers. Less so the child minders and the au pairs, he's old enough to be their grandfather after all. Hey, come on, nothing wrong with looking now is there? He's been DBS-checked and his record is spotless. He's scarcely going to do anything, hardly going to act on it. Just propagate some little narrative fictions in his head that's all. Even the mothers are of an age where he's old enough to be their father.

Come off it, one doesn't imagine the ancient skalds failed to get the pick of the women held enthralled by their storytelling prowess? Hard to credit that since they knew their work by heart same as him, they weren't casting sly shufties at the totty, in the guise of entreating them with whatever bit of the tidings at that juncture? Mind you, with the women all swaddled in layers of fur wrapped up against the perishing Arctic cold, not sure just how much of an appraising view the bard might be afforded. He knows the crybabies, (not to slight his present audience), the bellyachers and gripers are still tutting disapproval at him and his MILFs, mothers he'd like to fabulate. A little creative yarn inside his noggin is as far as it goes. He gets pleasure from a pleasingly pleasant gander. The mums get their kids right royally entertained. The library gets bodies through the door to boost its ailing case with local government. He gets paid by the library. It's all on a transactional basis and everyone emerges with a modest win. But he requires the garnish, the little cherry on the top, to do what he does. It may be money for old rope, but in itself it wouldn't be enough. Well enough perhaps only to buy himself some new rope to fashion a noose to put his head into, without this discreet daily perk.

Anyway, he never said which part of the women he looks at now did he? Jumping to conclusions there. Bit fast off the old starting blocks, all ready to carp and criticise. Just exactly whose mind is in the gutter here? Still, that's the social media generations for you. Net nannies with knuckledusters. Trolls don't only live under bridges, though those are the only type he engages with between the pages of a book. It's true the odd one might well whip out a breast to feed their sprog, but if the kid is here listening to storytime, chances are they're old enough to have been weened. Unless she's bred a brace in quick succession and brought them both. Anyway, fact is he's solely looking at their countenances. Fascinating studies of the differences in each fizzog. Those dowdily clad and wild eyed. Those insurgently coiffured but with bloodshot gazes. Those immaculately turned out and utterly unchanged as from before they sired. Will the progeny of the latter turn out to be better and more informed readers than those of the first cohort? He'd love to do a follow-up study to find out. Which of them reinforce the sessions here with reading of books to their children at home? Still not buying his attempt to elevate their censorious minds from cynicism are you? Well he does actually think about such issues. These are important questions. Keys to his vocation.

The passing on of knowledge. The future of literacy.

He raises that particular dichotomy, because he often stares at the women to try and hazard what if anything do they read? Do they restrict themselves to lifestyle magazines and coffee table books? He reckoned he could predict those by the pristine state of their manicure. Or, once they have their evenings back to themselves, finally restored the privilege of long hot baths, do they take up a book to engage with? And if they do, is it a book to escape into another world? Some bodice ripping romance, or pot boiler erotica perhaps? One unlikely to be shot through with the prosaic day-to-day tasks involved in childrearing at any rate. If that is indeed the case, do they inquire of themselves what is it about the prosaic day-to-day world that they feel they need to escape from in the first place? Is the choice of book a subconscious admission that this wasn't all quite as anticipated? That the received notion of the apotheosis of love, that of shared creation of a new life, doesn't quite scale the peaks of fulfilment? And what of those other type of books, the serious works of literature, the novels that do seek to engage with the world? Those which deal with relationships and desires and dreams and hopes? Regrettably they're seldom any better at providing solutions to the conundrum. Little in the way of transferable wisdom by which to live your life. For the only truth about fiction, is that it lies. Others may dub him untrustworthy and devious for his true predilections. Well he puts it to them that all narrators are no less unreliable. Just ask the bards. The ones with mellifluent voices and wandering eyes.

Dream Catchers

Amber had finished feathering the Photoshopped images of her collage, so that all the individual photos bled into their neighbours. A final anti-aliasing of the outer edges and her poster would be complete. She held her breath as she saved the file, transferred a copy to a memory stick and ran out of her house to the printers. "A3 size, hard backed please. How long will it take? That's okay, I'll wait. No, good idea, I'll go get a hot chocolate next door. Be back in an hour. Thanks."

She held the poster at arm's length. It was too adjacent to yield the effect she had worked for. She propped it against the monitor on her desk then retreated backwards, letting the frame of her bed intercept and chop off her motion at the back of the knees to seat her on the counter-pane. It was perfection! At that range, you didn't quite have the detail you did close in, but what you did have was the silhouette of W's perfect face formed by the edges of the photos. Seated in row 9 at the concert hall, he should certainly be able to see it from the stage and it would definitely stand out from all the other lame homemade efforts around her. She took a photo of it on her phone, then moved back in for some close-up detail shots and posted them on her Facebook page.

Annie, Amanda, Alison and Zoe were going off tonight to try and see the boys in their hotel. Twitter had been abuzz with which location they would be staying in prior to the Manchester gig. She used to go on such sorties herself, but was taking a break from them since as yet she'd never even caught a glimpse of them let alone got to meet them. Little point in a kiss chase that was all chase and no possibility of any kiss. She wanted a full night's sleep so she would be on top form for the gig itself. There would be a lot of screaming and dancing and she would need all her stamina. Her temporary abstinence was nothing to do with her Dad's cautioning her to do the maths. Ten million followers on Twitter, what were the chances that she would be one of the chosen (or 'lucky' as her Mum had amended) to meet them in person? She had hated him for reducing everything to that banal level adults reside on, but her comeback had come out all thoughtless and wrong as she had spluttered that the boys would have been nothing without them, The Fans, buying their records and magazines and going to the concerts. Dad had just rewarded her with an evil smile and a disconcertingly slow nod.

Anyway, it meant that only Abigail was around online. Well the others were too, but they were busy on Twitter giving updates on their futile quest to run into the boys. Posting out of focus shots of revolving doors and the barrier across a car park. They weren't really available to chat if they were totally wrapped up in their mission. Just as well really, since inevitably they would be jealous when faced with such a brilliant concept as her poster and look to copy it. But with the concert being tomorrow, they wouldn't have enough time. Not that any of them had Amber's skills and creativity anyway. You just had to look at their bedroom walls for proof of that. None of them could have cropped the photos so brilliantly to sculpt the silhouette of W's floppy fringe. After all, she was the only one doing GCSE Art. Abigail posted claiming she couldn't see his image in the collage, but she was just saying it because she was gutted she hadn't thought of it herself. Abi was always like that, wishing things away from her supposed friends, if she herself didn't have them. Were Amber or any of their gang to end up with W, Abi wouldn't be pleased for them, just bitch and moan hoping they'd split up double quick time. No way would W go with her, she has too ugly a personality. Just because the band produced that song worshipping all the unsightly parts of a girl's deformed body, most of which Abi actually possesses, she thinks it's a song devoted to her. As if! Besides, even if what Abi was saying was true, that could only be down to the small image her camera phone had produced. Anyway, push comes to shove, Amber was certain that Abi would ship Harvey more than W.

The rest of the gang must have been out chasing shadows till late last night, seeing as none of them were up and about and online when she logged on at 7am. No one had commented on her poster, presumably they had just stuck to Twitter. Stuck as in being glued to it. She could ping them a wake-up call, since like her they all slept with their phones, hoping to rise and shine after a visit from the Tweet Fairy having left them the prize of being followed by any of the boys from their personal accounts. She decided it was fairer to let them catch up on their beauty sleep. Abi was around, she'd posted a picture of her outfit for the concert. Not as tarty as Amber might have imagined. No, there was to be no negativity. Tonight's the night after all. Alicia from America had wished them all a brilliant gig and said how jealous she was, which was nice. She looked at her posterboard still propped up against her monitor. And then it struck her. Photoshop wasn't only usable for corralling celebrities and ideal men. She could use it to insert herself next to her beau. Pretend to the others that she had gone solo last night and actually been successful in her mission to meet W in the flesh. So she searched for the most lush image of W, which wasn't difficult seeing as he was always so perfect in photographs. Just once it would be nice for him to post a #justwokenup selfie on Instagram. She knew he'd still look flawless in it, but it would be a natural perfection, not one rendered by stylists, make-up artists and professional photographers. She gathered about six in a folder on her computer, which offered different possibilities for her own position in the picture. Head on his shoulder. Arm in arm. Singing a duet. Sadly they were all full-face on, so there could be none of him turning to kiss her on the cheek.

The problem inevitably, was finding the shot of herself. She lacked for stylists, make-up artists and professional photographers. She was podgy in so many photos. Her hair was lank, her skin puffy, or just discoloured. Bags under her eyes. Spots and acne. The list was endless. But though she lacked for a support crew, she did have *Photoshop's* airbrush tool. The pimples and bags were atomised away, (they don't call it a 'healing' tool for nothing). Her skin smoothed out into a single unitary complexion. She grafted hair from another photo on to this one to give it some life and body. Her gnawed fingernails were redrawn and manicured a wonderful purple hue. The transformation was complete. Now she started manoeuvring the photo against each of the saved images of W. Perhaps the best one was where they were stood next to each other, with W's hand draped over Amber's shoulder so that his fingers rested on her collarbone. A bit of *Puppet Warp* and W's arm elongates enough to spider down, so that his fingers now seem to brush her small bud beneath her top. Heaven! Except... again she wielded the manipulation tool, this time to exaggerate her breast. Maybe not so much exaggerate it, as bring forward its development a little. Then the other natch. W's hand was also thrust more into the foreground by the swelling behind it. It looked just a touch horror film. Her fingers hovered over the *commit* option. Her eyes darted from breast to breast, from that draped by W's sensuous fingers, to the bare one merely adorned by the fabric of her top. In the end she decided to revert to W's fingers resting on her collarbone and returned her breasts to their actual size.

However, this image was not to be shared with her friends. Even though that went against every rule of fandom, of the way the whole community was built, the dreams and love maintained through every shared nugget. No, this photo was just for her. A private moment, like a stolen kiss. She saved it to its own folder, behind a file name that gave no clue as to its precious booty. All in all it had been a pretty good start to such a big day. She consulted Facebook to check whether her gang were up yet.

Back off bitch! He's all mine

That was from Annie. She was probably her BFF. They called each other bitch as a term of affection. If it had been meant to be delivered with any real venom, then she would have used the language she does on Tumblr when she goes after those who attack the band or their fans. This was nothing like that. It would have been all capitals for a start. Somewhere she would have mentioned stabbing if she'd really meant it. She can be a bit OTT can Annie. Mind you, some of the boys she hangs with at school probably do carry shanks.

In yr dreams Amber!

That from Amanda. Fair enough. In all their dreams really. Oh wait, seems like Amanda's copping some grief.

Who won the band FB quiz? Not you part-timer plastic playing at it. I'm in this life 4 life

True dat Amanda, U're only into them because the rest of us R

I've seen them live more times than any of U lot

Only cos U got rich parents who drive u all over the country 2 see them

Whatevs. I'm getting a tattoo of Harvey. If I can persuade my Mum

Just go and get it done anyway. What's she going to say?

Yeah she pierced ur ears as a baby, so what rights does she have to tell U anything about how U want to look?

My Mum's okay, she likes the Boys. Says they're clean cut

Well she's a perv then. Seeing as she's TWICE their age

Only x2?

Yeah unlike yr Mum who is only about three years older than them

Alright girls, let's not fight. Not today

Yeah good call Ambs

Nice poster Ambs

Thanks Amanda. How'd last night go?

Pretty much a bust

If they were at that hotel, they ignored us as per

They couldn't have been staying there. No security men around

I'm sick of being blanked

They weren't blanking U if they weren't actually where U were

My sis gave me yet more earache about wasting my time and money

Bitch!

OMG! Didn't she use to dress up as a boy wizard and stand outside book shops at midnight just for a new Harry Potter book?

ROFL yes!

Anyone heard from Zoe this morning? She went off before the rest of us last night

Probably spotted some boy she fancied

No way! She always gives it all that, talking the talk, but she's defo still a virgin

Fo' sure. One of lads at school called her on her offer & told her go on then, put her hand on his cock & pull him off. She ran a mile

C'mon Annie, don't spoil the day by being all grimy and that

Why, it's true isn't it?

Whatevs. Just not today huh? Let's keep it perfect for tonight. Best night of our lives it's going to be

Only if I get a snog off W

Or one from Harvey…

Either will do me

Lol, Slut!

Gonna go & sort out my outfit for tonight

Me too Ambs

BRB... in about three hours!

I'm going offline to save my battery for tonight. Laters ladies

K Annie. Good thinking

Love all U hunnybunnies

Love U 2 Ambs!!!xx

Maybe, but not as much as I fucking love W.

Lesions of the Damned

After his parents split up, his mum was in the habit of dropping Jordan off at his gran's whenever she was working an evening shift. Jordan couldn't think of anything more boring, since his gran didn't have a games console and only Freeview on her telly. Mind you, having him round was probably no less boring for her. Although thinking about it, she never left her armchair except to make him his tea, so his presence seemed to have very little impact on her routine at all. Sat there, doing her dumb jigsaws. Almost as unmoving as the picture on the front of their boxes.

He asked her what the point of doing them was. She told him it was to build up the picture. He couldn't see the point of that at all. If she already had the picture, why did she need another one? No wonder they were called puzzles. She added that it gave her a sense of satisfaction to complete it. It also kept her mind from seizing up. Well that last one he could sort of understand, bored witless in her living room with its cabbage, liniment and general old people smell. It might have kept her mind from seizing up, but he could see that it did nothing for her twisted, gnarled fingers struggling to move the pieces around on her table and pressing them home to lock in to one another. She said it was the arthritis.

What was so great about these pictures that was worth having two of anyway? Boring scenes from the countryside, of ducks and swans on ponds, of horses in a field, of an old church (but no sign of any graveyard with wonky headstones), of a train going over a high bridge, some rowing boats and a sailing ship on a lake, even stupid puppies sat in a basket with a ribbon bow. There was one of London, with a double decker bus, but it looked like a scene from forty years ago judging by the clothes people wore (not a set of Beats headphones in sight). And each one came accompanied with a story she told. Not of the puzzle itself, but of something in it that had been personal to her in her life. The time she had been on a boat with gramps, or a train she had taken to be evacuated to the countryside during the war. Taking his mother to feed the ducks when she was his age. Stories of riding horses and walking pet dogs. She recounted these tales without any hint of sadness in her voice, even though they were all long gone from her life now, sat here hunched up in a chair. Maybe the puzzles kept the memories alive for her. Maybe she had to piece them together detail by detail in her mind afresh, each time she tried to recollect them.

One day she appealed for his assistance. Her hands were shaking particularly badly that afternoon, so she was having trouble picking up the individual pieces. She said she couldn't find one particular part of the sky and could he help her? He spluttered how was he supposed to find something that was all blue when there must be millions the same? (Okay, slight exaggeration on his part, the box said a thousand-piece jigsaw). She indicated the gap between four pieces of sky that she had put together. She said the shape was unique for that piece from all the other pieces that were also just blue sky. Jordan located it immediately. Wow, how did you do that so quickly she asked him? He just shrugged. Beginner's luck she decided. Since he found it, she offered it up to him to fill the hole by placing the piece in among its neighbours. He had to admit there was a certain sense of satisfaction, hearing the snap of the cardboard, obliterating the snatch of the tablecloth pattern beneath and forming a now unbroken plane of blue sky. She requested him to find another piece, the next one to fit on to that patch of sky. He did it in double quick time again and didn't wait to be invited to press it into place. She explained how when a piece slotted into another, that was called mating and squealed with delight as she said it. Jordan looked bemused. She tousled his hair and said he was a real demon at it. He reckoned it was similar to the pattern and shape recognition he had to do all the time in shoot 'em up video games, to tell friend from foe in the bat of an eye before you got dropped by a hail of bullets. He didn't volunteer this explanation to his gran though. Instead he asked her if there were competitive jigsaw tournaments like there were for poker and eating. She replied that she didn't know, but there was probably a Guinness World Record and that with a bit of practise he might have a good shot at it.

He began picking up pieces and slotting them effortlessly wherever their gape lay, as if they were calling to him to bring them home. His gran harrumphed and plaintively asked him to leave some for her to do. He apologised but she said he could get one of the other puzzles from the cabinet and do a jigsaw himself. As he sorted through the pictures on the front, trying to judge which one had the most blue sky, she instructed him that the thing to do was to find all the pieces with one straight edge because that must mean they were part of the border. If he built up the border first, then it would be easier to fill in the centre. He came back to the table bearing a box with a picture of kids flying kites, which to his mind had a satisfying swathe of blue, even if the kids themselves looked like annoying idiots. She informed him that was one of her hardest he had picked for himself. He lifted off the lid and tipped the pieces on to the table, careful to keep them separate from her puzzle tiles. His eyes scanned the heap, where some of the pieces had tumbled with their blank sides showing and just began bringing pieces together. He ignored her advice for starting with the border first and instead built out from the approximate centre of the puzzle. She watched open-mouthed, forgetting to carry on with her own picture. He completed it without pause and she brought her hands together in a feeble clap, but one which still hurt her hands he noticed. Think it's time to get your tea on, don't you? While they were sat eating in silence, the pre-cooked meal seemed more gristly than usual to her. She had the sensation that the morsels had taken the form of jigsaw pieces and the tabs were catching in her throat.

On every subsequent visit, Jordan sat down to blitz a puzzle in parallel with her more sedate progress. For each selection he made, she repeated her story attached to the image on the cover, though he noticed little changes in detail from the first telling when she had done the puzzle under her own auspices. It didn't really bother him, he was feeling warm from this shared activity and her words just drifting over him in a pleasant way. Soon enough he was on the last box she had available. She had got it out on the table ready for his arrival. What she didn't tell him was that she had removed a piece from it. She wasn't entirely sure why she had done such a thing. Was it a test? Did she want to see his reaction to not being able to finish, a feeling and an exasperation she herself had experienced on many an occasion? Maybe it was just devilment on her part, a reversal of their ages and assumed roles. Or maybe she was just jealous of his seamless ability. No, it wasn't about the difference in their dexterity. Just what jigsaws seemed to stand for to each of them. For the partially constructed puzzle with its yet-to-be-housed tessellations, represented to her the human brain with chunks gouged out, where former memories and the emotions associated with them resided. Only that could explain the relief on completing a puzzle. Only that could attest to the terror at the prospect of a puzzle going uncompleted, with its clefts and furrows, the teeming mental hollowing out, which lurked somewhere just over the horizon. How might he react at just a single such lacuna?

When he came in he didn't even remove his coat but piled straight into the inchoate mound of tiles. His fingers moved at their habitual dizzying speed, when he was suddenly stopped up short. He cast his scanning eyes over his bank and even parted some of the heap flat with his hand. He froze in place, but his eyes were still rapidly skirting over the layer. He informed his gran that there was a tile missing. She almost had a heart attack. How could he possibly know that? How could he mentally count a thousand – or rather, nine hundred and ninety-nine pieces – so rapidly and so accurately, just by sight? Truly he was possessed. She swallowed her discomfort in an apoplexy of apologising and tut-tutting at her carelessness for losing a piece. She offered him the chance to choose a puzzle of his own, that they would go down to the library straight away and select one. The library he queried? Indeed, that was where she got most of her fresh puzzles. He should get his coat on. Oh silly her, as she realised he was already wearing it. She struggled up out of her armchair to squirm and wince into her own garb. Once down at the library, Jordan was weighing up between a map of the world done as a jigsaw, or one of the Apollo space rocket. He plumped for the latter because he was drawn to the expanse of black, featureless space that eclipsed even the blockish mass of the blue sky in his imagination.

It took him less time to complete the puzzle than the walk home from the library, although his gran was an awfully slow walker with her stick. Each time he stopped to let her catch up, he regarded the cracked and subsided paving stones and thought of them not unlike a puzzle, with crazy angles and irregular interlocking with one another. The grey slabs merely lacked for a jigsaw's pixelation, except where sweet wrappers, crushed cigarette packets and flattened fizzy drink cans lay. Back in the parlour after he'd rapidly completed the rocket, he tipped it all upside down and broke it up again. He went through the heaped ziggurat with great deliberation, making sure all the pieces were face down, so that there was nothing to distinguish any piece other than its lineation. He then proceeded to reassemble the puzzle in this blind way. There was the pattern of the picture, but that was too distracting with its colours and images; for then there was also the pattern of the shapes themselves. This seemed to him to be a much purer assemblage. His gran was aghast at what she witnessed unfolding before her eyes. She thought he might have intuited her personal symbolism of jigsaws and was mocking her with this blank canvas representing a brain fully effaced by dementia. Or worse, that it depicted his own void mind.

But Jordan hadn't finished there. For his pièce de résistance, once again he broke up his flawless grey rectangle and turned all the pieces back over to their printed side. Then he proceeded to put tiles together. Since it was with the same speed as normal, initially his gran didn't see anything different even though her heart was full of dread. But when the image started to come together through the volume of interlocked tiles, she noticed with horror that now he wasn't even joining correctly aligned pieces together at all. He was forcing tiles together that didn't belong to one another. Having to employ pressure meant this was the slowest she'd seen him operate. The image that slowly took shape was one of utter chaos. As if the rocket had exploded in space and tiny fragments shot out in among the blackness along with stars that had blown up too. Now she knew for certain that he was not mocking her, rather depicting the likeness of his own mind.

Art Ache

Art tells no stories. Art is static. Fixed snapshots. Even Kinetic Art. It has no forward momentum. No narrative. By the same token, Veronica does not gauge the entirety of Christian art, with its symbols and tableaus drawn from the Bible, to be stories. Even though few could read in those days and relied on icons and stained glass, the paintings themselves still do not relate a tale in her eyes. Rather they reference already existing monographs in the Bible. Those canvases would mean infinitely less, without the explanatory code of the Old and New Testament. Essentially a gloomy-hued set-piece, amounting to not even an anecdote or a vignette. Illustrations. Grand illustrations granted, but illustrations all the same. Some berobed bearded guys gathered, pointing around a woman with a child sat on her lap, gurning at the viewer for all he's worth, while owls/doves/winged cherubs prance about around the perimeters. No, not prance, hover in place. Besides, such pictures were likely in private patrons' collections anyway. Not on offer for contemplation by the common man.

Art deals in light, colour, texture, composition and perspective. Ways of seeing. How we view things and how that vision constructs them. The manner in which the eye prefers certain things over others and works to fill in the gaps to its satisfaction. The geometry of aesthetics. The brain's inclination for pattern, arrangement and order. Even if artists have to counterfeit it through their tricks of perspective. Prejudicial preformation, all reality being like a painted stage flat. Veronica had no time for any of it really. Other than maybe Cubism. That did possess a sort of movement to it. She liked the way that it at least tried to show all angles simultaneously, the whole picture warts and all. And what did it produce in the works of Picasso? Freaks. Freaks behind primitive masks. Says it all really.

Art solely offers stories through the lives of its artists. Tales of excess, of real-life muses, economic straits and struggles while producing future multi-million dollar canvases. Fairy tales in many ways. Confessions through art, and lives lived on display. Veronica veritably has a couple of artists' stories for you. Lived out in private, under the roof of an unremarkable family home. Nothing gaudy or flamboyant. Merely that of her parents. Two artists who married one another and conduct a domestic life together, much as the majority of other couples who aren't quite so rarefied of imagination. Perhaps in some ways it's like the conjugation of a couple of actors to each another, or two shrinks. A shared vocation, earnest criticisms of one another's work, discussions of the latest exhibitions (to which she was unfailingly dragged along in her childhood). Dinner parties with fellow artists, agents, gallery owners and none outside of these occupations. A hermetically sealed world in which it is impossible to breathe.

Since Veronica had not been brought up with any stories, however much her parents might contest that claim.

Her mother is a fine artist. By which Veronica was not making any judgement on her mother's abilities. She paints landscapes. In acrylic. Pastoral scenes. Of a sort. Look closely enough and you see the fruit mouldering on the trees. Insect pests colonising the crops and other little suggestions of rot and decay. A lost Arcadia, though whether this was a personal forfeit for mum surrendering her childhood roots by moving to the big city to wed, or a depiction of the countryside's own evolutionary vicissitudes, Veronica has never been certain. If the former, then it is yet another artist's dreary personal statement of some aspect of their life. However, if some great howl about the economic and cultural decline of the countryside, then her mother has misjudged the nature of the medium delivering her commentary. Fruit rots on trees if it's not picked. It's just the cycle of nature. The very essence of the countryside she wants to uphold. No allegory to be derived. Nothing to see here. Her fixed frame of reference is unable to show the change over time. From growth, to decay and back through growth once again. Manet did, sort of, as he shone a light on the changing nature of, well light. So it wasn't any morphology of lilies nor any other pond life he depicted in transition.

Funny really, the etymological root (words are very important to Veronica, since she had sought out books {without pictures} as an antidote to the visual assault exclusively surrounding her in the family home) of 'acrylic,' is from the same word that 'acrid' is derived. By reason of the same noxious chemical being what is present in onions and garlic which brings tears to the eyes. Fostered, prompted tears, how very appropriate. Tears derived not from what the eye sees, but from a physical spur. Reflex tears. Chemically refluxed flow. What Veronica particularly likes about words, apart from their ability to construct stories, is that they endow her as a fine critic of art. There is the relationship of object to object on the canvas, how they are arranged in space. But then there are the hidden relationships, of chance, hazard and unstated, unseen power. Words allow her to shine a light on these, things that the canvas didn't formally represent. Words provide movement. An effusion of meaning.

Her father on the other hand, her father… His personal story inevitably demands an airing, not that he'd ever grant it such exposure. He is not a fine artist. In both interpretations of the word. His chosen material is metal. Thin, hunchbacked elliptical strips. Braced between two low-lying bases. Worked and worked and worked to death. By drill, angle-grinder, metal shears, nibblers, anything that could tear apart its very molecular structure. Yet the metal's burs are not only left untreated, but celebrated for their vertebral angularity. The surface of the metal is bubbled and etched by acid, but not with any patterned design, perish the thought. Rough-hewn for the sake of coarseness. Stained steel. The texture is as if corroded by rust, but it remains imperative that the steel retained its metallic grey sheen. What could be more soulless an art, than things wrought in steel? These sculptures are like fence palings of decay. Warped struts holding nothing together any longer. Misshapen armatures with nothing left to connect. The crazy-splay of joists when a concrete edifice is detonated and demolished, bowed in supplication before an absented draughtsman, divine or secular. These are not the blight of mum's faux-arcadian vistas, but the disintegration and degeneration of the industrial world.

And what are these visions of jagged archness supposed to convey exactly? Despite the obvious associations with inanimate structures and erections, this is actually a figurative art. He is forging representations of people. Stick-thin antitheses to the bulbous, warm curves of Henry Moore and Barbara Hepworth. Anorexic art. Under-nourished art. Starving artist art? More like a representation of concentration camp survivors, of which father had been one. 'Die Musselmänner', skeletal labourers in the camps until they lay where they had dropped. Sights somewhat formative for stamping the tender eight-year old imagination. (His she meant, not her own. She grew up with them from a far earlier age). Not that tight-lipped vater/pater ever uttered his precursory inspirations in any interview, or critical retrospective article. His sleeves perennially rolled down to cover up his tattooed identity. The Musselmänner who accepted their fate and completely shut down until it fell upon them. A passive symbol of protest from her father? Far from it. This is his revenge. This is human flesh imprinting back upon industrial metal. Flaying it to within an inch of its mineral life. His art is the Quisling Fifth column inside plush skyscraper offices of today's equivalents of IG Farben, Krupp and Flick. For these multinational conglomerates were almost exclusively her father's customers and clients, until the bottom fell out of the economy forcing his retirement at the never-was ripe old age of eighty. Only just as with her mother, Veronica adjudges that he misconstrues his metaphors. For all the murderous intent, this isn't any flesh's revenge, simply the onslaught of metal tool upon metal recipient. And while even she could admit of the excitement at a girandole of sparks being raised by the onset of a speedily revolving cutting blade, her father is shrouded behind a welder's mask, his entire body encased in a protective armour. Not a jot of flesh on show to proclaim its supposed triumph. And the receptions and meeting rooms containing father's pieces? They subvert nothing of industrial capitalism, only silently accumulating value, further feeding the system. The narrative doesn't add up. Sorry, flow.

There is repetition aplenty at play, enough perhaps for a designation of obsession. But this to Veronica's mind does not constitute pattern. And certainly not one of any regularity or orderliness. At least mum's works are restricted to the walls. Dad's colonised all possible floorspace, anywhere child Veronica might have fancied stretching prone in order to play, or curl up with a good library book. Lacking for toys, play consisted of a disconcerting version of Grandmother's Footsteps, standing in relationship to a sculpture, positioned on one side seeing convexity, turning round and seeing it as concavity. An impromptu assault course in the parlour, still snagging her leggings and grazing her all too exposed flesh. The inside of a giant whale in which she has washed up inside. The thorny belly of a leviathan. Hmm, maybe not. How could her sea-based metaphors compete in her parents' realms of the catabolic bucolic and the agonised mechanised? Yet there are inextricably three dystopias within the household. None of which communicate with either of the others, for all her parents' stabs at honest appraisal of each other's work.

So what is Veronica's own story? One she necessarily had to construct for herself. Certainly she knows where it ends. And she hates herself for it. For succumbing to the prevalent iconography. That which she fought so hard against. Now bouncing between hospitals, clinics, halfway houses and isolated therapeutic communities. From slaloming a path through distorted bodies cut from steel in the parlour at home, to here, with a profound body dysmorphia of her own. Though non-artistic, since she absolutely does not view herself as a work of art. The irrefutable truth, how ultimately the visual sense cannot be outranked by any of the others (save in the oh so fortunate blind). The imagination cannot successfully erect bulwarks against what the eye takes in. It has its presets. The visual cortex processes along pre-defined templates. And like a replicating virus, it uses the imagination against itself. Veronica knows it is absurd to seek for her body to attain the dimensions of her father's unyielding Musselmänner. Her strabismal imagination each time she looks into a mirror, offering only perspectival legerdemain. Alice, Snow White, King Richard II, the Lady of Shalott (onions make you cry with acrylic paint leaching out from your tear ducts), Dracula and Dorian Gray, none of them could save her now with some redeeming alternative looking glass narrative. Besides they were forever and in perpetuity, engaged dealing with their own issues. Of course as her counsellors forever counsel, there must come a time in one's adult life when one stops ascribing the blame for one's actions on the parents. In the same way as her father had to stop ascribing blame to the camp torturers (difficult when every day starts with remarking on his tattooed wrist as he buttons his sleeve to cover it up). In the same fashion as her mother ought to stop pining for some rural idyll which she left behind, or which left her behind. Read Faulkner or something of the like, there is no majesty in the countryside. There are no stories in visual art. Only snapshots. Fixed, framed and frozen in time.

His Goal

Zack's mother measured his growth by making him stand by the jamb of his bedroom and marking the level of the top of his head with a Sharpie on the painted wood. Zack always protested the rigmarole until he himself realised he could cast his own height by reference to the football crossbar. At Under-7 level, neither he nor any of his team-mates could reach it even by jumping. As they progressed through the next couple of years, they could merely stretch up a hand to first rattle and then fully clasp it. Some even clambered up on to it and produced amusing monkey impressions, until Coach shouted at them to get down. A pre-match routine more faithfully adhered to than the warm-up stretches they were enjoined to execute. Then they moved on from seven-a-side matches to nine-a-side and they were once again dwarfed by the new set of goalposts. And so began the incremental process of closure of the gap all over again. His Dad on the other hand, reckoned his development through meting out targets each season; of goals, assists and man-of-the-match awards. Zack wondered how a boy could even be considered for a 'man'-of-the-match award.

As the goalposts changed in size, so too did his father expand the dreams Zack was to shoot for. The inducement was always the latest in football boots. His first pair of studded boots had been a thing of beauty. The bright orange design, the coloured flashes, the soft leather that gave to the slightest touch. His Dad had bought them for him ready for the start of his first season playing for a Sunday League team. His Dad had sunk to his knees to slip them on his feet, then inclined himself to tie his laces in a double bow, like on a cake box. And so it was before each match, pitchside in all weathers, there would be his father prostrate on the ground, genuflecting over his laces. Consequently Dad's track suit bottoms were always muddier than Zack's own knees, as if his Dad had played in the match too. He didn't realise at the time, but his Dad had displayed a similar reverence for the ritual, as had the priest at his church when he put on his vestments in the sacristy, while Zack and the other choirboys donned theirs. Zack no longer attended church, since the Sunday morning kick off times for services clashed with those of matches, much to his mother's vexation.

But the boots no longer stayed immaculate. First there was the buffeting they took just through fulfilling their function of shodding the feet that kicked the ball. The leather became scuffed and scratched, worsening as winter wore on and the wetness imported from the grass dried out by the radiator, creased and cracked the skin. They were no longer soft and pliable, more like a hospital plaster cast, as his father had to ram Zack's foot into the unyielding hide, often causing him pain. Finally, after his mother taught him how to tie his school laces, his father also ceded his own oblation at Zack's feet. He reasoned that the rest of his team-mates were doing up their own, so therefore Zack wouldn't want to look any different and come across as more childish than them. This impeccable logic fell short however, when the referee had to blow his whistle to stop the game for Coach to come on to the pitch and retie Zack's unravelled laces for health and safety reasons. It was only to be Coach, for certificated child protection reasons.

After the joy of a hot bath to scrub off the mud, followed by the shared communion of watching the afternoon's live televised matches, every Sunday evening was spent scrutinising the online page of the league his boys' club played in. Listed were results, goalscorers, man-of-the match and on the team's individual page, the whole squad and the number of appearances each had each made. While Zack led all categories, he always felt sorry for those with a big fat zero in the goals scored column. They were all defenders and therefore less likely to break their ducks. He felt particularly concerned for the goalkeeper who had no chance of registering a goal, even though he rivalled him most closely for man-of-the-match awards. This had so nagged at him that during a recent match, when Zack had been fouled and awarded a penalty, he had sprung back up and called for the goalie to be allowed to take the kick. There were howls of dissension from both Coach and his own father stood at the touchline, so that Zack was still charged with the responsibility of taking the kick. After the match his father ticked him off for making such a suggestion and at the next training session, while Coach never mentioned the subject, the goalie came up to him and said that his own father had reckoned that Zack was well out of order for offering such a gesture. 'Patronising' the keeper's father had pronounced it, even though neither he nor Zack knew what that meant. However they were both fully versed in the other choice word, since it was the one frequently used by Coach after a defeat; 'humiliating'.

Zack couldn't understand why there had been such a strength of reaction and neither could his mate the goalie enlighten him any further. But he did appreciate that goals and the other statistics were immensely prized, like those Gold Coin players that were almost impossible to land in his console football game. The penny had probably finally dropped, on the occasion where he and his fellow striker both arrived at the same moment to connect with the ball and fire it into an unguarded net. Both boys just grinned inanely at each other in the face of the strange occurrence. But their cordial confederacy was interrupted by a disturbance on the touchline where both their Dads were being held separated at arm's length by Coach. He could see the vein pulsing in his father's forehead as he swung his arms into the buffer space that separated them. They were both laying claim to the goal on behalf of their respective sons, to chalk up another notch in the goals' column. Coach was demanding of both men what kind of example they were setting, while the Referee had removed his notebook from a pocket and was making a note in it. He jogged over to the two boys and asked them what their fathers' names were. As he jotted them down, he informed them with a wink that the goal would be one for the Dubious Goals Panel. Zack only found out later that no such thing existed in the junior Sunday league as it did in the professional game.

On returning home that day to his mother's usual cheery inquiry from within the kitchen as to how they'd fared, his father gave a curt "fine" before heading into the lounge to turn on the television. His mother took this to mean the team had won but Zack hadn't performed terribly well, which wasn't in fact the case. Rather her husband was banned from attending the midweek fixture that had been rearranged after the weather had done for it earlier in the season. The other father would also have been banned, save that they needed his car to help transport the team to this away game. Zack's Dad was currently disqualified from driving so had no such mitigating circumstance. He was spitting feathers, since he had already booked the day off work in anticipation. Now he would have to spend the whole time at home, getting text updates from one of the other fathers, having to scroll through all the eulogising of their own son's performance first. Zack trailed into the lounge after his father, who spun round and with thunder etched across his whole face, spat "Scouts look at those pages online." Not the cub scouts of unfashionable uniforms, triangular proficiency badges and bandanas strangled into cringeworthy woggles, from which Zack had been spared due to his football commitments, much to his mother's vexation, but the mythical beast that was the talent Scout from professional clubs. He who lurked and hovered at Sunday league youth matches and who all the dads spent the pre-match warm-up by the boys, trying to unmask from the gaggle of spectators dotted up and down the touchline. The Scout who could confer not eternal life or happiness, nor the hand of the queen in marriage, but the eternal riches offered by a professional club's football apprentice contract.

Zack had undergone a trial with a professional club already. He'd hated every single minute of the experience. Firstly there were the dimensions of the pitch, being full-sized and designed for men, not fourteen year olds. Then he had been told to play in defence, something he'd never had to do before. He managed to query it with his Dad before the match started and he breathlessly offered him that the club wanted to see his versatility, (which his Dad had to go on and explain what the word meant) and also that he could follow instructions and not cause problems, because they wanted to test his character to see if he was a team player or not. Zack had accepted that even though he felt that for the first time in his life he was not an automatic first pick, more like the fat or speccy kids who were always the last to be chosen by the captains drawing up their sides in the playground. An impression further emphasised when he saw the size of the strikers he was up against. There seemed to be no strict age segregation here, no one had to provide their photo-identity cards as proof of age unlike at Sunday league games. Many of the boys here with him at the trial had to be a couple of years older than him at least. In the ensuing game he'd been run ragged by kids with longer strides and greater speed. He'd been clattered by telescoped-legged tackles that he'd never had to calibrate against before, while he himself bounced ineffectually off his opponents' muscled bulk when he tried to contest for the ball. And he never won a single aerial challenge for want of giving several inches to his adversaries. Both he and his father had sulked on the train journey back home. What he didn't realise was that his father was not brooding over the injustice of the ordeal that had been put before Zack, but that rather he had apparently failed the test of character the challenge had put before him. "How much do you want this Zack? How badly do you want to become a professional footballer?"

That night they had gone online to see how his league

team had fared during his absence at the trial. Zack's heart sank when he saw that they had lost, but his father seemed to regain some of his usual chirpiness when he espied that not only had the team failed to score, but Coach had presumably been suitably unimpressed so as not to award anyone the man-of-the-match accolade, not even the goalie. "No damage done son," smirked his father. "You're still miles out in front and no matter what happened today, no one can take these figures away from you. There in black and white it is, for all to see."

"Dad, is your playing record there as well then?"

"Ha no chance! Back in my day we didn't have the internet and no one can be bothered to go back all that way and load up our stats. What would be the point? No one's scouting for old geezers like me," as he flashed a wide smile at his son. It was later that night after a few cans of beer sat in front of the televised matches, when his Dad admitted that he wouldn't have had much of a record to transcribe anyway. He would barely have merited a mention. The sole confession in a day of conspiratorial silences and evasions. For when his mother had come in demanding why Zack was sat watching the match instead of doing his homework having been out all day, his father without turning to face his wife, had piped up that he himself had overseen Zack do the homework on the train journey up. Seemingly placated she left the room and his Dad gave Zack a sly wink. Somehow it was a touch more sinister than that given by the referee over the disputed goal.

Yet Zack had not been entirely freed of his chores that day. After an in-depth discussion of wing-play based on the televised evidence before them, his father had sent him out into the garden to practise. Zack hated playing out wide on the wings. Having to run the gauntlet of hectoring fathers. Hurling abuse with flying gobs of spittle and pulsing protruding veins in their foreheads. (Zack ruefully wished the attending Dads also had to demonstrate proof of their age given how they behaved). You didn't even get any relief when you switched ends at half-time. Scooting down the touchline in front of your own team's Dads could be more intimidating than those of the away side's. At least there were no such terrors out alone in the garden. He began his mazy weaving runs around the Spacehopper, a tricycle, the Swingball pole. His father had rigged up this slalom course to test Zack's mettle, no longer now having to beat imaginary opponents he couldn't envision, nor avoid being blocked by non-existent antagonists. All fashioned from toys and games from his earlier life. Zack's mind drifted from his dribbling drill ('dribble', such a strange word for such a technical skill of control as it actually was). Instead he contemplated whether these toys had been stripped from him by his own natural course of development and maturation, or whether his father's overweening ambition had prematurely retired them from his childhood and repurposed them for this. Whose restless need to move on did this represent?

Another letter arrived from a different club asking Zack to attend a trial. "I'd rather play for the team I support Dad." It was slated for the day after Zack's next Sunday game and his father's return from his disciplinary suspension.

"This is a proper good club Zack. Not like that other mickey mouse outfit. Several of their players have gone on to play for England. Think of it son. The chance to represent your country. To play with the crest of the three lions on your chest. Do you know anyone in your family or friends who's done that? That would put you in a very select group of people, a special club that everyone will look up to us for. It doesn't get any better than that son. I'm telling you."

"If I get chosen for their academy, will I have to move away from home? Change schools, move away from my friends?"

"Course not lad. You'd travel there evenings and week-ends."

"But I couldn't keep playing for either school or Boys' Club?"

"Probably not. But this will be an altogether better standard of football. Different level altogether. And you wouldn't have to take the train yourself. Mum will drive you there."

"She hates football. What's she going to do while I'm training?"

"She'll be watching you of course! Proud as punch as I would be. She doesn't hate it. Not really. Not if she stops to think about it. What it actually means. You can't pass up this chance son. It's too good an opportunity. Life changing. Set you up forever it will. You, me, and your mum. You've got to grow up a bit and appreciate just how good this is. I never had any such openings as a boy. Didn't have the ability you have. You've got to maximise it. Not let it go to waste."

Zack went upstairs and sat on his bed. He put his palms to his eyes and just held them pressed there. He wasn't holding back tears. He wasn't fighting back a headache. Nor was he trying to rub some perspective into his clouded vision. When he was finally confronted with the impression of the blood coursing through the vessels in his eyes, he queasily relented. Zack rose from his bed and went over to his chest of drawers. He took out his England football shirt and examined the crest. There were what appeared to be three badly drawn creatures which didn't look much like lions. Or if they were, they had been rendered by a ten-year old. Only if it had been by such a young hand, then all three lions would not have been reproduced as flawless copies of each other. Zack was not au fait with heraldic iconography, but he knew enough of modern mass-production to realise these were not hand drawn, but industrially reproduced.

He reached around in the drawer for another England shirt for comparison. Zack had a plentiful supply, since every Christmas present was an England shirt and every birthday was a shirt from his club side, with seasonal regularity. The result of tramlined, pedestrian thinking from his parents. Or his father in all likelihood. This drawer was full of such shirts, with geological stratification to mark each year's minor changes in design used to lure the purchasers and fool them into believing they were distinct and genuinely new. No child could afford to be caught dead in an old shirt (their catechumenal irony sensors being too underdeveloped to allow for a 'Retro' look), so slavishly each season's fresh design was gobbled up by gullible parents. And indeed, each new shirt did seem to consign all Zack's previous year's experiences to history. That none of it counted for aught, as he moved a further rung up his proto-career ladder. The only grain running through each year, every strata of his life, was the game itself. Actually, even that wasn't the case. New Coaches, different ideas, diverse methods. The game became more incomprehensible, with too many tangles of things to hold in his memory when he stepped out on to the pitch. Only the hectoring of the Dads, stood watching roped one metre away from the touchline, remained the same.

He found last season's England top. He propped a hand

under the badge of each shirt and brought them to abut each other. They were identical. So whatever the other alterations in the design, the badge remained unchanged. The sole link to its heritage. That and the lone unblinking gold star. To symbolise having won a solitary World Cup. Some fifty years ago now. All that hope and expectation of adding a second and further stars beyond, remaining unfulfilled. They had never again escaped their own home atmosphere to blast off into the stellar realm. That was too much pressure heaped on each generation of professional footballers, to bring home the ultimate laurel wreath. It had crushed many a player and every manager, the weight of a whole nation's demands on their hunched, rounded shoulders. He was not sure he wanted to enter the select club mentioned by his father. To become yet another member humbled and stooped like Atlas, not through the burden of the whole globe, but just one tiny mouthy island on it. He threw both shirts back to splay languid and lifeless in the drawer, until his mother came and refolded them neatly while he was at school the next day.

After the midweek game played in the clear space created by the absence of his father, Zack had made his mind up. Today was to be the day. The last opportunity he would get before his upcoming trial. He had to get everything absolutely spot on. He had to convince everybody. It was a shame it was an important top of the table clash and that he would be letting his team-mates down, but he could no longer see any other way through. Perhaps he would be able to help them get far enough ahead in the game so that what transpired thereafter wouldn't wreak any significant damage. But so far, the opposing midfield worked relentlessly to cut off his own team's supply of the ball to him. While additionally he was well marshalled by his opponent man-marking him tighter than his own shadow. Imagine that, one fourteen-year old boy 'man'-marking another fourteen year old. Still, he was flattered that seemingly their opponents had trained with him specifically in mind for this match. By half-time he'd barely had a kick and his greater plan was seriously in danger of being left unrealised. His half-time orange tasted particularly tart as he played over things in his mind. Coach upbraided him for not stamping his authority on the game, but he didn't even hear him. It was only when Coach threatened to substitute him that he got his head right and snapped back into the moment. He was helped by his father's bawling out of Coach for even daring to suggest such a thing as to remove the team's best player and their only hope of winning the match. Coach bent down and put his hands on Zack's shoulders. He then looked straight into his eyes and Zack shuddered that he could intuit there his real intentions.

But he was sent out to resume the second half and within moments was able to seize his opportunity. As the pass was played for him to turn and run on to, he adjudged that his marker was going to be fractionally late getting to the ball. As he nudged the ball diagonally round, he proceeded to drag his foot to clip the outstretched foot of his would-be tackler, sending them both sprawling. Don't roll, don't roll, just drop like a dead weight and let the ground receive you so it looks realistic. Precisely as he'd practised for hours on end against the scarecrow toys in his garden. Just as he'd studied on television, those tumbles referees fall for hook, line and sinker and those they don't, which always involved rolls. He didn't get winded by the impact of the ground as he hoped, probably because it was too soft, so instituted plan B. He got up, buckled his leg away from him and immediately collapsed to the turf again, holding his knee while letting out a blood-curdling scream, even though it was his own plasma that was quaking inside his veins. He knew this manoeuvre was the hardest to fabricate credibly. YouTube had limited footage. He rolled and pivoted on his pelvis, both hands immediately clasping his knee. The bemused defender approached him and as per the F.A. Fair Play mandate, offered his hand down to Zack to serve for an apology. Zack rammed his eyes shut and continued rocking from side to side, his knee raised from the grass gripped between his hands.

Coach had reached him by now and plonked the first aid kit down on the grass. He waved off the opposing player's still extended hand of friendship, so that he mooched off to go take his place in his team's defensive formation. Coach encouraged Zack's hands away from his knee as he gingerly began to flex the joint. Zack conjured up the tears that he had been practising so hard into his bedroom mirror. His Dad had now caught up to them and was hectoring Coach to leave well alone since he could be doing more damage. Coach angrily responded that he held the requisite medical certificates, but that cut no sway with his father, who brushed him away as he scooped his son up in his burly arms and marched him off the pitch, striding like a colossus bearing a fallen comrade from the field of combat. An intimate heroism only disturbed by his father craning his neck past Zack's ear resting against his shoulder, to inform the entire world and his wife congregated at the park, that his son had a very important trial with a professional club this week. Zack snaked both his hands round his Dad's neck, partly to accentuate his own sense of vulnerability and helplessness, partly to delicately winch his father's attentions away from the pitch. "Dad, I felt my knee go. I know I can't put any weight on it. I've no chance of making the trial tomorrow."

"Don't worry Zack, hot bath, bag of peas on the joint, keep the weight off it and a good night's rest. Actually no, straight to bed after the bath. Put a pillow under it. We'll have you back on your feet in no time. I knew we shouldn't be turning out for this rabble. Way bigger things on the horizon for us son."

That was no good for Zack to hear. The one thing he didn't want to have to do, was to repeat the buckling act under the scrutiny of professional players and coaches. "Dad, I think it's more serious than that. I'm going to have to get it scanned at the hospital."

"Okay son, we can do that. I'll drive you there right now. Sunday morning. Hopefully shouldn't be too much of a wait in A and E."

When Zack closed his eyes this time, it was a genuine gesture. He was basking in the closeness he felt to his father, both emotionally, as well as the physical proximity. This was recapturing that feeling when his Dad huddled over him to tie his first boot laces all those years ago. And he knew this would be for the final time, probably ever, between them. For any scan would inevitably show there was not a whit of damage to his knee. That he was perfectly fit and healthy, certainly there was no reason he could not make his trial. Then even his father would have had to realise that in faking, Zack's true bent was set against progressing his football career beyond today. He had encountered the opponents and they were way more physically imposing than a Spacehopper and Swingball pole. Hungrier too, none of them could he imagine cooking up such a scheme as this, even as an idle fantasy, let alone going through with it. He had experienced the bilious abuse of twenty spectators around a pitch, which had proven more than enough for him, let alone that of thirty or forty thousand in a stadium. Through that one moment of a counterfeit dive, all his Dad's dreams for him would have gone for a burton. They had discussed the morality of diving many an afternoon sat in front of the television. His father felt it dishonest and cheating and against the spirit of the game to the very marrow. And yet when Zack had put it to him that he might be the player, the England player in a World Cup Final, who dived to win the decisive penalty, what then? His Dad had come round to an acceptance in the case of his own son. Zack's heart had skipped when he heard his Dad say such words and right now he really needed to believe that principle was irrevocably true. That he could forgive him for absolutely any transgression, right? But he knew this was now a wholly different ball game. The dive back there was designed to finish his coltish career before it had really started and all the shoot dreams it betokened.

He couldn't even just return to playing with his mates, for they too would be mortally wounded by his treachery towards them. There would be no more replica kits at Christmas nor on his birthday. No more new boots when his feet had grown beyond the dimensions of the current pair. No more adaptations of multifarious objects in the garden to set up football assault courses and establish imaginary foes for him to best. All that along with the trust, love and ambitions of his Dad would be gone. But none of it mattered. Besides, perhaps he had discovered a new, proper calling. Given his performance back there pitchside, maybe he could develop a career in acting. Hollywood actors were maybe even more famous than footballers. Plus they used stuntmen. There was plenty of money to be made there. If you reached the very top.

Marta Martyr Stigmata

Marta was born with a port-wine stain birthmark on her face. Though disfiguring of her features, it was held as an auspicious talisman by her agrarian community. Wine-brewing folk, fortified by their faith in god. (Not for them any Bacchanalia honouring the intoxication of the grape. They tirelessly trod it under foot as if it were the spawn of the very Devil himself they were charged with exorcising). They took Marta's blotch to be a sign that their vines would forever fructify, since the hue of her blemish was exactly that of the infant grapes they grew.

However, the sons and daughters of the farmers were far less permissive towards Marta. They teased and mocked her for her ultramontane pigmentation. Some brazenly tripped her over so she toppled head first into the soil. Then they blotted her face in the loam, trying to scour her nevus off against the grain of the earth, or just interring it beneath the grime. Marta couldn't reconcile their reactions towards her, set against the awe and indulgence shown to her by grown-ups. The adults refused to take their children in hand and remonstrate with them which further confused her. In this village it seemed as though the children wielded the power and the adults remained hapless and helpless bystanders.

So Marta's skin flared and raged by way of response and sirening alarm. She developed the coloration skills of a chameleon, though it rendered her no protection of camouflage. In the presence of children, the rest of her face and exposed skin of arms and legs blushed to match that of the original imprimatur. That only made things worse for her of course, but it was something she had no control over. It was intimately attached to the shame and self-disgust these children made her feel. In the presence of grown-ups however, the rest of her skin would remain normal, though the port-wine stain itself would darken during the season, as it matched the ripening and maturing of the grape. This naturally made her seem even more portentously anointed to these simple peasants, though a few secretly wondered whether she was a witch, toying and aping and scoffing at what was their most precious value after god himself. But none dared bring their fears out into the open.

And thus did the village spin on through the cycles of the harvest. When Marta's first menses struck, her skin chemistry moved on apace once again. Now in the presence of adults too, her whole face could darken to the hue of the stain, for no seeming reason. Such a blazoning of livid purple-red was augmented into further indecorousness, by a puckering of her skin at the forehead. Her poor mother and father lay in their marital bed discussing the forlorn prospects of their daughter ever having suitors, notwithstanding that they were cheered at the prospect of not having to provide a dowry. They resolved to discuss it with the village priest, though they were sly enough to dress up their concerns behind the question, of whether their blessed daughter was actually elected too sanctified to marry a mere farmer's son.

Yet Marta's skin resolved the issue in its own animated way. With the catamenial had also come fantasies. Fancies over men (not the hideous, persecutory boys). Woolgathering over some of the farmers, working with sweated torsos out in the vineyards. She had no one she could confide these feelings in. No one to console her as to whether they were as natural as the ripening of grapes. But her treacherous skin divulged it to her. And thereby informed the rest of her village. Every time such a lascivious thought entered her head, her port-wine stain would tumesce and throb. Radiating her thoughts like a balefire. The villagers didn't catch on at first. They were just initially perplexed by this new fleshy encryption. They feared it might actually presage a contagion striking their shoots. Or a pestilence settling upon them and sucking the lifeblood from the precious fruit. But when their vines continued unmolested, they peered harder at what Marta's own blight might be signalling.

Of course it came about that it was their seed who provided the first key. For they were in the habit of staring at Marta incessantly, in a manner that the adults could not afford, seeing as they had wholly to succumb to the pulses demanded by Nature and head for the fields. The children however discerned that when Marta's affliction struck, she was pointedly looking at some adult or other. And not just any adult, but always a male, usually himself pigmented by the exertion of his labours out in the field under the hot sun. They could not believe their findings and for once were careful not to shoot any premature bolt without rigorous evidence.

Yet in time they came to be certain of the empiricism of their senses. The mechanism of their discovery disseminating throughout the whole village wasn't clear, but leak it did. Soon every inhabitant knew what her darkening shading betokened. "Dirty thoughts." "Immorality." "Unclean and impure." "Rude, lewd and disgusting", even though they themselves had their own similar arousals, merely they were able to keep them hidden beneath the gristle of their skin. They proceeded to subject Marta to an inspection of her hymen to ensure she hadn't acted on her impulses. Women hurled invective every time their paths crossed, or they spat at her. While the men recoiled at the thought of her maculated face coming anywhere near them. Though contrary beasts that they were, they also felt slighted if they weren't one of the objects of her desire beaconed across her flesh.

Less and less could Marta walk the village for the opprobrium cast upon her. The childish goading of her peers was now nothing to that of the adults. "Polluted." "Foul-minded." "Filthy, sordid mind always in the gutter." "Indecent and sinful, her mother must be mortified," "Profane and corrupt, her parents must make penance for engendering such an obscene creature." "Don't even look at her children, or you could be infected by the taint of her disease." "She is the work of the devil."

And so they hung her from a tree as a witch. Some said her port-wine stain throbbed and pulsed in pleasure as she twitched and writhed in the noose. Their grapes fructified on, though their colour was never quite as rich as previous generations.

*

None of the parables, allegories, apologues or fables offered up by mother and grandma, not those of ugly ducklings, frog princes, beauties and beasts, rags to riches, even those of their own inspired invention, could ameliorate Martha's troubles. Of course not, they were fictional and therefore inapplicable to the real world. A world where Martha was being bullied by the other girls. Where on reaching puberty, she made herself promiscuously available to the boys, in the belief she would at least be popular with them. But the boys being boys, used and abused her, while her ready incontinence only inflamed the ire of the other girls further. The ubiquity of social media allowed them to hound Martha even when they weren't forced together in the environs of school. They exhorted her to remove herself from their lives. Permanently. Martha hung herself in her bedroom. The symbolic distancing 'truth' of the universal stories, could not outblast the concrete unanimity of chorused voices, that were all too proximate in her everyday life.

Sophiastry

Mum, I truly honour you for instilling in me a love of books. But the love of reading I secured all for myself. Having deduced certain compressions embedded in our collaborative reading practises. Since they failed to reveal me to myself.

You did not ordain any book to create a magic circle around us. Like that of a genuinely reciprocal discourse, as they did down at the library, where we kids all sat on the floor transfixed and drawn into the power of the story by the teller. Nor was I offered the magic circle of just me alone, inscribing the invocatory power as my lips traced the words across the page as happens now. Rather, you configured a stenosis of private intimacy, excluding everyone else in the world. Emptying the whole universe just for the two of us. Having christened me after you, whenever someone entered the room and addressed one of us by name, we are both behooved to answer. Yet whenever you or I pronounce the name Sophia, (well just you really, since your other connate soubriquet was 'mum'), it was clear and distinct to whom it was applied. A one-way broadcasting channel. Our convoked trinity, me sat there on your lap, book in that hand free from the other enveloping me against falling, was totally prescriptive. You were sermonising me.

So now I appreciate while we were sharing many moments, we were not usefully sharing what was being read. There ought to have been three minds propped at your knee, mine, the author's and yours, as facilitator for me and the book to become thick as thieves familiar. But you nipped and tucked to augment your role. More chaperone than matchmaker. The book was reduced to an instrument for enhancing a chatty colloquy. This was more cosiness than genuine intimacy. A bosomy burrowing, rather than a journeying outwards into the book and through that the world beyond.

You painted pictures for me from the text. Your pigments were words, so that your paintings were somewhat circumscribed. The lexical equivalent of stick people, box houses, a circular sun with spokes radiating outwards and trees with two branches and a handful of leaves. The sort of thing I myself was coevally etching on to paper in stubby crayon and which was pinned up on the fridge. But you weren't mirroring my mind back to me. You rendered neither of us service when you tried to bring yourself to my level of interpretation. The tree is stunted, the sun hollow to its core. I'm sorry to relate, that though you are an adult, your imagination has become clenched, whereas mine is still lithe and limber. Or maybe merely yours is in temporary abeyance, through being in thrall to words. No, no, I think the palimpsest of you can be overwritten no more. Your personal parchment has so dried and cracked, it cannot be rubbed clear again to receive any fresh content. Your body of words has petrified. It precludes the engagement of my iridescent inspiration.

It's not your fault. It reflects how you have to move through the world. It is the reverse of Adam and Eve and the Tree of Knowledge. Eating one of your apples shutters my eyes. Sugar-coated pabulum to draw the sting of life and make it sugary sweet and unchallenging. Do I wish to ever grow up into such a diminished state? I don't know yet, the cost-benefit analysis is yet to be conducted. But I know I have no desire to enter it right now. I have too many investigations yet to prosecute. I know it seems a contradiction, since I am myself trying to parse words in books, which is not necessarily the same as responding to the real world. Yet what else do we have for structuring our thoughts but words? I am on the upswing of expanding my critical vocabulary, whereas you are on the down curve, well beyond any crisp, innovative analytical cusp. I have to process books through the playpit that is my imagination. Let the images prance and caper, see where they lead me.

For under your tutelage, these books do not accord with my own senses. The admittedly provisional findings about how the world is. As attested when I turn my eyes away from the pages and take in the evidence of my immediate surroundings. The divergence is less about that from the books, which I know to be conjuring magical worlds anyway, but more the marginalia and explanations of them that you gloss. For example, it is patently never 'happy ever after'. There are plenty of times when either you, me or dad, or even collectively, are far from perdurably 'happy'. That takes care of both 'happy' and 'ever' in one fell swoop. And as for 'after', well when they lowered Grandpa's box into the earth, there has never been an 'after' for him since. Although Grandma has perked up considerably from that point, which again speaks to the mutability of 'ever after' as remarked on previously. And even post-maturation beyond the level of fairy tales, you still importuned me as to what I thought happened to the characters beyond the final pages of the book. Why always this preternatural haste to get to the end of people's lives? Is it something to do with Grandpa again? I was never terribly interested in the fate of the characters beyond the pages. I was involved with them there and then. In the here and now of the book's lifespan, the duration of its reading. They were dead to me beyond that, but very much alive while I cogitated on their actions as described by the author and recounted by you (we'll come back to that particular part of the dynamic anon).

And then there is the notion of what lessons you wanted such fictions to inculcate in me. The moral centre of such stories. That cheats don't prosper? When clearly it seems that they do, such as that inveterate agnostic Mrs K who started attending church services just to secure her scion a place in the church-run nursery. Her daughter was not a happy bunny about having to surrender her Sunday morning diet of "Countryfile" and "The Week in Politics" (alright then, cartoons followed by more cartoons), to go sit on the cold wooden pew I can tell you. The first day of the new nursery intake and Mrs K's rotund form never again blotted out the streamers of light through the church's casements. Or that so long as one says 'sorry', people will forgive your misdemeanours? Funny how through sleight of words, people elide that into claims 'it was an accident' or 'they didn't mean it', which is not quite saying sorry now is it? I have found folk to be anything but pardonable, resolutely holding on to their grudges and being utterly vengeful. Empirical evidence backed up by my own reading material. Even if there was some sort of reconciliation and redemption by a book's end, I used my own critical senses to draw more judicious conclusions about human behaviour.

Mater, you concretised the abstract for me and I well acknowledge that was your job. To conduct me into the seasoned world which you and dad and all adults occupy. Acculturating me to personhood. Domesticating my imagination into the serviceable. So much for your intent, but I find that I am bound to question your methodology to even be able to deliver these explicit goals. Let us return to our former trinity at your lap. The reading convocation inevitably breaks up when you got up to brew yourself a revivifying cup of tea, or me some sustaining gruel. Leaving me unattended with the book to ponder and process what we have just read. And this was heartily encouraged on your part. Yet at night we sundered one from another during the very same reading operation. Me, lying horizontal in my bed, a corner upon which you were perched. Signal of rather a different function of the book. To convey me into sleep and away from the roil of musing upon the preceding daylight hours. Moreover, any further reflection on the text being read to me, is curtailed by the flick of the light switch plunging me into darkness. Under the covers prohibits anything further between the covers. I am to ransom the extant glowing moment of the book and its story, for sleep. Save for the possible permeation of distorted readings of it entering my dreams. And though I may reach for the book myself on waking the next morning, the excitations aroused by its sentences the previous eve are lost to me by then. Riddled through the colander of my brain that necessarily concentrates all its energies into refurbishing me afresh each morning. That I am the same little girl Sophia, with the same basic, tentative thoughts and comprehension of the world, as I was the previous day and that I hadn't changed wholesale into some completely different beast. Novel bookish vistas could not be factored into that calculation at such a tender juncture of the new day. Otherwise my brain would be the same steamed mush that you serve up for my food.

I have however, devised a stratagem to overcome this information loss. I read it in a book. I was going to secrete a candle from our power-cut trove and ignite it under the sheets to enable me to carry on reading without discovery. Only the hidden location of the matches so far has stymied that solution. However, a different plotline has furnished me an alternative rectification. I just need to come by a torch to wreak the same illuminating affect. Now, if I can just cozen daddy into buying me one. A little bit of being scared of the dark ought to bring about a favourable result. The oldest trick in the book.

A Briefing on Time's History

Twins Vincent and Harrison were auspiciously, (or synchronously depending on your ontology), prematurely born under the sign of Gemini. Their mother believed in astrological determinism, their father believed in differentiating between his sons in order for them to individuate. Their mother dressed them in matching co-ordinates. Their father surreptitiously changed an item of clobber here or there to try and distinguish them one from another. Not to facilitate his own powers of discrimination, but to try and foster theirs. So that they were not confused by staring at their twin and misconstruing it to be looking in a mirror. A sort of inverted Lacanianism. Their mother cooed and trilled in the general direction of her sons, which usually meant petitioning the space between them where they lay supine on their mats. Their father was very careful to address his words directly to one child, before turning to address, usually the same message albeit phrased differently, to the other. Thus the mathematical equations engendered by the nodes of this neuclidean family, were somewhat beset by a set of variable congruences. First there was the perhaps psychically bonded pair of the twins themselves, though at this rathe stage they lacked for a means of articulation of any such linkage, being barely conscious of their own singular selves. Then there was the mother-father pairing, each pole very much out of kilter with the other of the dyad. Finally there was the triangulation of mother to both sons and the parallelogrammatical father and sons axis. This was taxing geometry to be sure.

So much for spatial relationships, the temporal seemed warped as well. While the twins' own nascent sense of a sustained existence took the expected time to bed in, the comings and goings of their parents, together with frequent supplantation by a nanny, meant they hardly seemed either sequential or persistent. More sort of episodic. Stroboscopic. And yet as the scionese twins waxed on a bit further, now time seemed eternal. Days of endless playing, punctuated only by fuel stops. (The weather may have determined the locus of their play, which in turn prescribed its fashion, but no climatic conditions could proscribe and preclude play itself). It was only the cozening of the night-time story paternally read at their bedside, uniquely involving a unitary address to both, that lulled them with its prosaic prose lullaby into finally forsaking the frolicking. Yet when Vince woke the next morning all that was forgotten, as the ludic possibilities of the day once again reignited him to seamlessly inhabit its consecutive moment. However for Harrison, instead of playing with his toys, he earnestly fingered the nighttime codices, to try and pierce their dislocating power that had stopped up his uninterrupted being and brought it to a summary cessation the night before.

Some nights his tormented thoughts meant Harrison

couldn't sleep. That the transformative thumb-sucking thaumaturgy of the book had not worked in its entirety. Such capricious and incongruent patterning only made him more want to penetrate the occult lore unleashed by the various nocturnal grimoires, with their simple line drawings and no more than two rows of typeset incantatory magic per page. Nevertheless, he was afraid that to turn on the bedroom light would alert his parents. Nor did he want to disturb the evidently untroubled sleep of his twin. Instead he rose from his bed to stare out of the window and look at the night sky. Gazing upon the twinkling stars, he matched the never-ending continuum of time, with the limitless scale of space confronting him and thus began to conceive of the possibility of infinity. The infinity of possibility. Nope, neither were registering with him as being in accord with the reality of things. He had no confirmation for his findings, just his place in the universe felt asymptoteamatic. He credited himself just like one of those shining stars, trying to compete with its lustrous broadcast against that of all the others. One tiny, insignificant point of view, dwarfed in this huge canvas of rival claims. He looked back again at the sleek, unpinched features of his brother in repose. How Harrison envied him. Well may Vince continually feel as eternal as the heavens at this tender juncture of his existence, but doubt had entered Harrison's being and was gnawing away at him. He couldn't help but feel a nagging notion that someone was spinning him a line.

None of the primers he had read, informed him that looking out there upon the firmament, he was encountering another fiction. One with no more veracity than the planetary mobile erected above his bed (his brother had an animal one, a disparity at the insistence of his father).

For the light he nightly encounters is eons old. It could very well have emanated from a star that is no longer even in existence, just the report of its death is yet to reach his earthbound eyes. He doesn't realise it, but what Harrison witnesses is akin to the cosmos's family album. Sepia tinted shots from past eras, of the longest exposure. Evidence of stellar mortality having been airbrushed out of such a record. Even if the star persists, it has not yet completed the task of transmitting its light to him, so that still he was never currently in the moment of the star's contemporaneity. Excised by the fractures of time. Akin to one of those unoccupied seaside photo-shoots, with a painted wooden scene of caricatured bodies in old-fashioned beachwear and holes for the real flesh and blood faces to protrude through. The whole matter called for further and more in-depth research. Something a tad more sophisticated than *The Tiger Who Came To Tea or We're Going On A Bear Hunt*. Even if there was both the constellation of the Great Bear and the Little Bear. That was coincidence. Synchronicity, nothing more. After all, there was no 'Tiger' constellation now was there? Try as he might, the code would not yet yield its abstruse arcana to him. The act of reading merely served to take him out of the immediate present. Immersed in other worlds, ones shrouded in the inverted dark of black print upon white page, unaware that the author was possibly long-dead just like the stars. Transmitting the illumination of their words, which have yet to expire, but unable to add any further gloss of exegesis to them from their grave.

But in time, Vincent caught up to Harrison's apprehension that temporality and in particular their own lives, did not stretch unendingly boundless. That the segmentations of school, then work, marriage, plus raising one's own kids (at least in Vincent's case), serrated their chronology. It also segregated the pair of them, as Vince met all this with a cheerful ataraxia. He felt neither cheated nor rationed, but ploughed on ahead regardless, relishing all of existence's bounty. Life's exigencies only constricted its limitlessness a scintilla or two. But if his brother was all blazing skyward luminosity, Harrison was the gnomon on the sundial casting parts into shadow. He still continued to read voraciously, trying to unlock life's latencies, but the other parts of his being were eclipsed, paralysed, frozen into ataxic inactivity. If his brother looked life full in the face and planted a smacker of a kiss on it, Harrison shied away and inhabited a penumbral realm more akin to restive quietus. Just he and his books. The books that continued to misrepresent to him, like an unfaithful mistress, yet which also like a mistress, he could not part from in vain hope one day of matchless requitement.

Harrison thought back to the very genesis of his tribulations. The wellspring of words that had so plundered and spirited away the futurity of his time like the thief of the night. Actually, night itself was the thief, which was why he stayed awake through the darkness on sentry duty, to protect against any further larceny of his being. Though even his own nocturnal patrols through the literary canon could not spare him from dozing off as light came up for the dawn. The illumination of the words on the page slipped from his grasp as he succumbed to slumber. The thievery baton had been relayed over to morn, while he had drowsily dropped his own. Manifestly the time of day was not what was accountable. Harrison had what he thought might be an epiphany, though it could conceivably have been grand mal epilepsy, what with all the high velocity conjectures bagatelling around his head. Perhaps the enchantment had not been evoked by the printed words in the primers, but through the voice of his father reciting them? An invocatory sympathetic magic. No wonder he could not now settle to anything with the long ago passing of the old man. But wait, hadn't the incantatory bewitchment offered up by his father, been different for he and Vince? Had those divergent words shaped both he and Vince's characters like golems?

Indeed, his father had been largely responsible for his own language. Seeing as how his mother had cast her words into a no-man-or-tot-land somewhere between he and his twin, like first aid packages plopped into a war zone, bursting open on impact, or being whisked away by the belligerents bearing down on the ragtag partisans. How he had initially assimilated language through repetition. Recurrence. Regularity – ha! His labour one of mimetic patterning. Fed by the grown-ups, mashing up words into phoneme gruel. Made palatable by sprinkling sugared crystals of syllaburble, caramelising curdled word strings. And thus do children take this language in order to order their thought into legibility. To make known their desires to their providers for calorific fulfilment. Yet as Harrison could attest to, the mind is not always orderly. Far from it. Some thoughts are fleeting, mind motes one attempts to pinion and pluck from the neuronal spaces, but misses, or they slip from his mental grasp in his eagerness. Sub-lingual spoors of being, which have osmosed into the alkahest chemicals in the developing tray, but not condensed over into the photographic image staining the paper. Instead only left with a lancinating pang at having been unable to bring them into the light and make it legible. Double, multiple exposures hovering over into regret. Transmuted into frustration. Emotion, that which mainly resides in the realm beyond the lingual. This is the primordial lack. And why he Harrison, and no doubt countless others, try to recapture it, to enflesh it, by resorting to the ideational hunter-gatherers of the species. The raven mavens and the cracked experts, the writers who try and tease out their excitations and perturbations. They who comb and panhandle and frack and salvage their own minds for nuggets of expression. For affect to bleed, from in-between the words. For each novel provides a personalised stations of the cross for mental contemplation and ordination. Yet Harrison finds himself left empty. The metal husk of a skyscraper yet to osculate the sky. A Gaudi cathedral without windows, lacking for any stained-glass pictorial narrative. Books lie to readers. Fiction lies. Over and above the partial disclosure of themselves as fiction.

Vincent died what was held by all to be a good, if somewhat premature death. It was deemed to be good because he expired surrounded by his loved ones, his face unblemished by any lines of tension, with the pain medicated away and he didn't soil himself even once as he remained in possession of all his faculties. However, unsurprisingly as an identical twin of the same genetic make-up, it was the 'premature' element that Harrison fixated on. He rapidly moved to submit himself to a battery of pending medical tests and probes to check for signs of the same corporeal flaws that had accounted for his brother. (In time none were detected, but rather than providing relief and reassurance, it merely injected the role of chance and happenstance into his calculations). Harrison recalled two balloons they had been given for a formative birthday, their names lovingly if asymmetrically spelled out on them in glitter by their mother. The balloons had been of surprising quality judging by the duration of them remaining inflated. But eventually Harrison's had sufficiently degraded to surrender its air, while Vincent's carried on robust and tumescent. That had bothered Harrison at the time, balloons from the same batch, presumably filled with the same cubic capacity of air at the nozzle of a mechanised pump. And yet for no good reason one had outlasted the other. But it hadn't turned out to be an accurate portent. Vince, not he, had terminally deflated. 'Premature', who is to say when something happens earlier or later than expected? That depends on both the expectations, but even more significantly, it came down to the scalars of time again. If one didn't have any expectations at all, then time ought to be eliminated from the equation. If one had no concept of time, it was impossible to be in possession of any expectations. For when would the reckoning come?

Harrison considered his brother's life. This was not an act born of altruism, but because he'd been asked to deliver the eulogy. He only knew of panegyrics from books. Somehow he had to apply that to talking about a flesh and blood human being. Not a fiction. He attempted many different structures to hang the armatures of the speech. A chronological framework seemed the most natural, but it was made lopsided by a more intimate knowledge of his twin when they were children, from that after they went their separate ways. He looked for patterns to his brother's life, mileposts marking out stages of progress and development. But these seemed opprobrious to he who lacked for them all himself, while equally his brother had blundered through the customary and the mundane without any significant thought or preparation, rather just letting them descend upon him as they would. An unspectacularly solid work life of bringing home a wage packet to put a roof over his family's head, feeding and clothing them, with enough change left over for weekend leisure pursuits attested by the family record of the photo album thrust at him sobbingly by his sister-in-law. The same recurring faces arranged around varying outdoor props, clad in differing seasonal outerwear. There was no discernible design at play here. Rather than pattern, this was collage. The fact-finding mission wasn't going terribly well.

His brother hadn't only had a good death, he knew by received consensus that he had pursued a good life too. But what in point of fact did that mean? Harrison knew it had been a touchstone question posed by the Ancient Greeks, one that had formed a foundation of philosophical thought thereof, but what did it amount to, let alone entail in these days of moral relativism? Beyond the broad blandishments of others, he really didn't have a lot to go on. If there were themes at play, he couldn't isolate them. Everything about his twin's life seemed to be repetition. Recurrence. Regularity. The three 'R's'. Just the very same as his own. Except in the adorning details. Consistent and characteristic of a- the- man pertaining as Vincent. Yet could they be said to have formed patterns? For they achieved nothing of importance or impression. Left no imprint on this earth. Hence though there existed these traceably predictable behaviours, if they led up to nothing of consequence, then any assertion of pattern could only have been as in decorative. Wallpaper, backgrounding lives lived in the background. This is why literature opted for heroes, demigods, semi-divines, those who rose above the human crowd by tilting at something over and above the banal. Naturally, with a whole panoply of fully paid-up gods as members of Olympus, the Ancient Greeks couldn't permit such upstart behaviour and beat them back down for their hubris. That was where the novel eventually diverged from drama, it allowed the possibility of benison, salvation, redemption for its flawed heroes. But where books held out the chance for a life of substance and signification within, reality afforded no such permutation. Wasn't it Jane Austen who modified the notion of 'pattern', away from its association with 'patron' and 'patronage' as something to be slavishly and feudally imitated, into one of decorative design in and for itself? From appetite to aspiration, a further hollowing out. The beginning of mass reproduction. Of tastes and dreams and consumerism. Something which does not call for its own duplication, nevertheless secures it anyway through an homogenisation in its beholders.

Harrison miserably failed to acquire the fundamentals of his brother's life. Said life just didn't read like that of a hero or protagonist of a novel. His brother had to all intents and purposes declined to undertake any journey, other than the imminent one in a hearse and its termination in being sunk into the ground. And was he destined to the same fate? At least his brother had left the borough during his family holidays. The same could not be said for Harrison. Born here, lived, if his existence could be dubbed 'living', in the same environs and likely to die and rot away under the same parochial loam. How could anyone live a story? Until they die, they continue to extend their narrative, in however paltry increments. It is open-ended, without a conclusion, until their death, whereupon someone else, a ghostwriter, appends the afterword and closing chapter. Just who would panegyrise the story of Harrison's life?

He concluded Vince didn't have a story. He'd never

approached his life as one, rather just lived it in the minute, reacting to stimuli around him. Going with the flow, whichever way the breeze blew him. Whereas Harrison had lived his life leeward. Yet through reading books he had only seeded a barren interior life. Nevertheless, there was one way in which fiction did converge with his own story. Time passing in the narrative of books equated to time passing in his own life. Real time lived in fictional unreality. Literature, not night, not his father, was the thief, stealing away his proration of time. Through the empty endeavour of reading stories. It was stories which were dilating him with their literary speculums, in order to scrape out his own gist. Expending precious, or not so precious swathes of his life. The characters in these books might pervert the passing of time by changing their presets, altering their behaviour, setting the metronome of their lives to pulse at a different frequency, to stretch and eke out further time, though only out of sight of the reader beyond the final printed full stop. Yet for him, the physical act of reading merely further enchained him in his familiar rhythms. Those which had ground virtually to a halt. Those that would have been difficult to register on hospital monitoring equipment. All lines are printed flat in books.

Overwhelmed by the grinding millstone of having to encapsulate the story of his brother's life, Harrison sheepishly handed the task back over to the presiding priest. The prelate, used to viewing people through the cross wires of confessional box gauze, looked directly into Harrison's confoundedness. He challenged him as to how could he not know and construct the life of an identical twin? Had they perchance been separated at birth, reared by different parents like some horrendous, immoral scientific experiment and recently reunited only to be cruelly rent asunder by such tragic circumstance? Harrison's blurted response indicated that he wasn't even acquainted with himself, thus reaffirming the cleric's initial reading of a man with an afflicted soul. He politely inquired whether Harrison might consider a trip to the confessional, but Harrison swiftly rebuffed the offer and further harrowed his own soul by berating himself for his seeming impoliteness in the alacrity of his spurning. On the day of the funeral, Harrison deferred to the priest's economical encomium to his brother. Arrayed chronologically, it set out a series of bland events that could have applied to any man, yet expertly seemed to fulfil the expectations of the assembly in the chapel of remembrance, whether they were intimately related to Vincent, or just associates. The priest had painted a pinpoint picture of nullity, just like one of those seaside photo-shoots. Only now of course his brother's head was missing, the hole for Vince's face remaining vacant and the light behind uneclipsed. It suddenly struck him as to how he had acquired such a metaphor. Unlike his brother he had never gone to the seaside on holiday. Perhaps he had seen just such a photo in Vincent's family snapshot albums. Or more than likely he had read it in a book.

Kissing Cousins

Neuronal Nodes engaged:

> Alien Neural Structures; Sense Perception; Data Processing; Communication; Language; Literature; Fiction: Science; Science Fiction; Biochemistry; Quantum; Biology; Progenitorship; Parole; Langue; Founding Myth; Myth; Futurity; Time; Integrality; Conceptualisation; Symbology; Reflexivity; Mental Imaging; Relationship to Other; Intentionality; Computational Processing Power; Incarnational; Internalisation; Paradox; Subjectivity; Delusion; Illusion; Renewal; Persistence of Being; Parallelism; Causality; Dimensionality.

*

One has observed your scribes stationed at their horizontal planes, graving on a second horizontal plane of delicate thinness. Yet once one has translated and absorbed the content of their striations, one finds them not to be chroniclers, chartularies and recorders at all. Rather they are engaged here in their very immediacy, projecting forward to future times. Taking them out of their present and often out of their own world. Your world. Only these scriveners lack for any knowledge as to when their communiqués will reach their audience, since each congregant (a word one has to settle on despite its imprecision, since these assignees of the writ do not congregate in any such manner but receive it in isolation), chooses for himself, or herself, when to consult the inlaid words. So ordinarily one would say, that must inevitably narrow the futurity of the message the scribes were aiming for. Only having studied the texts, which are so wide of the mark of encapsulating the prospective, that one has concluded that these are not predictions they produce, rather an inventory of current anxieties. The future becomes collapsed into a reflection of the scribes' very own contemporaneity after all. If the worlds depicted seem not to match to the ones in which they actually reside, that is because these mirage worlds are carved from the material of fretfulness and tension; distorting mediums upon the rational. What remains unclear is the true nature of these anxieties, where they source from and what their relationship to the scribes are, so much that they feel obligated to swathe and cocoon them within a misshapen chrysalis of time.

One has scrutinised all your depictions of aliens, monsters and extra-terrestrials and one can only but inform you, that you are light years discrepant. Further comparison studies by related nodes charged with such analysis of your planet's flora and fauna, once fed back to one, reveals that there is not a single example of these creations that does not derive from your pre-existing genera. Do your fellow planetary inhabitants pose you so much danger, that you constantly have to portray them in a perpetual state of war with your own species? Based on what evidence? You degrade them in word even as you degrade them in biota. Germane nodes have analysed the neural structure of these creatures and found them to be almost entirely hard wired in the manifestation of their behaviour. And yet the same cannot be said for your own species. You have an acceptable range of neural plasticity and yet these books are themselves like a petrified neural network. The sentences frozen axons. Your neural organs can barely hold together the notion of singularity of self. No wonder your scribes project into their works figments of a coherent character throughout. And one that additionally is able to undergo change in his perceptions about himself. They are trying to fight against the truth of your actual complete lack of mutability.

Collectively one has analysed this to be the inevitable outcome of sapiens' continual tendency to concretise everything, including yourselves, into a material form. One has not found any concomitant need to do the same. One extends through the environment of galaxies without any difficulties. Without substance, one has the same imperviousness as light energy. The same ability to transport anywhere unhindered. One can still observe and then report one's findings, without the need to chemically splice amino acids into proteins in order to manifest oneself to you. One does not need to resort to proximate presence and the use of analogue probes to download data from you, one's subject of present study, despite your scribes' bafflingly persistent representation of just such a process from peregrine visitors. These texts leave out so much, through the limited palette of what they do choose to depict, that one inescapably concludes this mirrors the functioning of your neural networks. Since one also does not have any imperative to reproduce descendants, one can foster more connections among arterial nodes. Which is what one does each time it encounters new data to assimilate, such as one finds currently through encountering yourselves. Though your peculiarly anomalous remedies for existence, have necessitated the dedication of many fresh synapses in one's network to try and pierce its abstruseness. But one still has the requisite capacity. One does not credit that the reverse would hold true. Not to judge by the testimonies provided by your scribes.

Furthermore, even though one has no notion of parenting as you do, yet fraternal nodes charged with studying extra-terrestrial intelligence have still gleaned that there is a most curious occurrence during your neural expansion. That for the span of two revolutions around your sun of any new sapiens life, there is a respectable growth of neural connectivity. However, beyond that span, further neural development is only one of sclerosis. The connections harden themselves through repetition and practise, as you assimilate certain functions, particularly the acquisition of language. Such capacity colonises the space where other more fecund links could have been forged. You surrender the infinite by doing so. Contracting your horizons, narrowing your ambitions. Presumably this is why the organ of your neural network is so wrinkled in its withered topography. One apprehends that this is due fully to your self-realisation in material form. That to exist corporeally, that body is necessarily disposed within an environment. And then you are challenged with surmounting and subjugating that environment. Else the body perishes. Oneself has minimal experience of death. For when one node corrodes and surrenders its electromagnetic energy to entropy, parallel nodes pick up and reroute the data firings, so that it becomes a source of new connections being forged, engendering further creative potentia. The sum total of information therefore remains permanently undiminished. Moreover, one's own neural processing power is not only puissant, but it is almost instantaneous. (This is an unimpeachable fact baldly stated, not a boast as it might be portrayed by the hand of one of your scribes). The neural network is the most complex, powerful entity throughout the cosmos. Yet yours scares you and your first reflex is to attenuate it through atomisation. Rather than recognising its own immensity as a network, each discrete body caters and cares only for its own existence. Its own persistence. And your scribes capture these hopeless struggles in their heterodox, aberrant manner, either wittingly or unwittingly, one is not clear on this point. (One additionally notes that you are not without models of communal neural networking within some of the lowly animals you deride as unthinking- because they are instinctual- 'hive minds').

Were you able to process at near the speed of light as oneself, you would see that the indurate perceptions you have based your reality around, do not hold fast at all. You might also benefit from the operation of quantum affects to not just forecast the probability of matter, but actually be able to apperceive its actual behaviour, since your neural processing would itself be quantum. However your biochemistry inhibits this, since it is in the service of your corporeality. Your scribes are not specialist creators, since each and every one of you who holds up the foundations of reality and indeed of his own identity, is creating a singular narrative, a mythology for himself and the world he moves through. And yet the contradiction is that for you to conquer the environment so as to flourish, you have to render it consistent and predictable to each and every one of you. Causality is clearly sequenced, so that human reactions are appropriate for overcoming any obstacle. Thus you have imposed a lattice of reality upon the material world and all perceptions are made to accord to a place on that lattice. Sense data is partial, one's analysis showing about fifteen percent, since you are only scanning for variegation and deviation from the visual template your network has constructed and already holds in place. Minor variance is smoothed out through the sense data being forcibly incorporated to match the existing template. Any more significant disparity, calls for action by the body within the environment to remedy it. This is why one states your perceptual apparatus is petrified. Your visual senses see the world in a way it has pre-evolved to interpret it. Your concepts of space, of directionality, depth, emptiness and mass, how all objects are arranged within the visual field, are determined by your biology. Then your neural networking brains go about trying to ascertain the rules behind these purported facts. Unaware that they are already enshrined in the inner map room on the walls inside your cranium. It is the same blind mechanism behind your drive to reproduce. That biological imperative already exists, you just adorn it with the justification of parenting, love, legacy and all other improbable, phantasmagorical elements your scribes enshrine in their volumes. If your anatomy was different, these rules would not be the same. Therefore reality, your reality, cannot be objectively 'true'.

If you still contest one's findings, that your reality is just a constant narrative you spin yourself, propped up through partial and pre-set affirmations of the sense data by the neural network, then consider this. There are wavelengths of the electromagnetic spectrum you cannot experience, again through the constraints of your biology. Though your brain has conjured ways to measure it, nonetheless still it remains out of reach of your daily perceptual apparatus. Yet another amputated dimension from your alleged reality. A stunted biology results in you being unable to conceive beyond four dimensions. Language, which struggles to relay the three dimensions in which you anatomically operate, utterly fails to communicate four. Where are the true (or even fantastically imagined) description of multi-dimensional worlds and beings like oneself? Your species needs to move beyond its current delimited vision. But until it comes to an appreciation of where that vision comes from, yourselves, it has no chance of standing outside itself. Only the ego-less neural network can genuinely cast beyond itself. Possessing the generative, imaginative power to conceive outside of, and greater than, itself.

One could maybe comprehend if these texts had been generated by your collective minds to stand as myths, for whatever purpose such myths were designed to inculcate. But no, these texts are originated by single individuals, to what purpose one cannot successfully isolate. And yet through further induction one finds that, after all, this is a version of a communal output. Since though your neural networks remain unconnected to one another in any comprehensive way, yet they are so similarly bounded by their own constructions, that there is an inherent shared capacity in what they can process and the output this generates. The starting point of what you deem to be your parochial reality. The problem being you have made yourselves virtually incapable of projecting beyond these notions since they are so all-encompassing. You are in need of new matrices for being able to break out of the smothering insulation of your puparium. But the books, these books analysed by one, through which you enhance and solidify your learning and your experience, are predicated on the circumscribed narratives sharing the same assumptive reality and the language that underscores it. Therefore it is self-reinforcing. A non-virtuous circle. One recommends that you require new schemata to tear down the walls of the brain's abridged narratives. Then you might be able to distinguish between the real and the fictive. You would have no need of symbols and metaphors to try and express things in such indirect ways. Your language could be made to fully function for you. With precision and exactitude. Instead you, that is each and every one of you and not just your scribes, reify symbols so that they oppress you. You put them out of reach of your own ability to truly comprehend them, so that they elude you. You make them both more solidified and yet more detached from you. Metaphor fortifies pattern, for metaphor finds the commonality between two diverse things related only synchronously and compounds them together through a casuistic parabolic alignment, providing a false symmetry and an inert resonance. Yet you take metaphor to reveal insight, because discerning new patterns equates to knowledge on your world. You would be well served to stop believing you project your creative output outwards, such as in the form of books. Because your inceptive act was to provide the inner map, the topography and reference points of your neural network. Look inward, penetralia not marginalia. Recognise fiction for what it is. A retardant on your development.

After one has delivered you the prudence of one's insights, one will reclaim most of the neural capacity expended and reallocate to one's next circumstance in the galaxy. This is one's customary process, but one must append that the receipt of your information caused some perturbation along various nodes of one's own neural network. To the point where one wondered whether through contact with your species, one had contracted a virus. Implanted these lurid and outlandish notions that blend and merge conceptions of reality and fiction. Were you in fact attacking one, using super-subtile fiendishness under the guise of fatuousness and derangement, to parasite one's superior processing receptors? It was the cause of some considerable analysis and computation on one's part to see if there was a real threat. Even one's tyro science-fiction node struggled to perceive if this was a synchronous embodiment of the science-fiction trope, in which case fiction had again blended and merged and become confused with reality. Or whether what one took for science fiction was in fact an actual happening, whereby the human race was manipulating reality to make one conceive that one was merely a character or a plot entity in a work of fiction, as part of the struggle to dominate and control one. The energy surge entailed by such ratiocination, degraded one's connections and processing power, so that one's lights will go out soon and one's data will be redistributed elsewhere. However, one's final assessment was, that given the limited scope of the reality that you had confined yourselves within, this was most likely to be a case of science fiction with corollary confused boundaries, rather than any hostile inroad. Therefore, one has left as a recommendation to one's coaxial nodes, that if your planet were to implement one's suggested course of remedial evolutionary action, then in the future one might return to update one's information on your planet and species without fear. But one feels it will remain a matter of low priority, that one's specialised study of fiction will naturally be retained, only demoted to deep storage within the neural network. For, as such an outlier with regard to knowledge about existence, sapiens' version has little insight quotient contained within its data.

Treatment

I know it can't keep going on like this. That I have to bring about some change in my life. I can't carry on living through books, with my nose continually pressed down between the pages, instead of holding my head up to gaze back at the world outside. So much so, that my blackheads aren't filled with begrimed pus, but with printer's ink! No? You don't appreciate how much it even takes for me to get out my front door to come here. So far removed from my usual routines. Yes, routine singular. I have most of my needs delivered via online ordering. Food, toiletries, a few clothes and of course my books. Agoraphobic? No I wouldn't say that. It's not a spatial thing. It wouldn't bother me if I was stood in a big open area. Just so long as it was denuded of any other people. You know Sartre's 'L'enfer, c'est les autres'? How others loom up in our consciousness and potentially affect and distort our sense of being? Well, I have largely immunised myself through my stylite lifestyle, albeit at ground level.

But incontestably a few cracks are beginning to show.

Loneliness? Not really. You're never alone with a book. I know, that sounds trite even to my ears. Like an advertising strap line. Let's say more that books are my companions through life. But yes, within that there is ineffably an element of solitude. But then I read these books and witness others engaged in disastrous and destructive relationships, so maybe being among people is not all it's cracked up to be either. But I'm essentially reading to peruse what lies between. Between how they conduct their lives and how I live mine, a veritable cleft between the two. Relationship, conflict, love, jealousy, betrayal, forgiveness, redemption and so on and so forth. Since so many novels produce the same basic parameters, utilising these fundamental building blocks, that many authors can't be wrong can they? One can only presume that they must be broadly writing from their experience and that experience seems rather far removed from mine. So I read them to try and figure it out for myself. Well, yes it is fiction, but it must bear some relationship to the real world, otherwise why would we read them? Not just me, I mean other people. Different mentalities other than mine. It must speak to them on some level about their own lives? For all that it's fiction, the emotions aroused must be true wouldn't you say?

That's the thing see, the study of the protagonist in the novel, opens up vistas for all humanity. From the individual to the universal. Freud would have approved of that dynamic, although from the other end of the telescope, using universals to get to the core of a single person. I believe it was explored by him in *Civilisation and Its Discontents*. What, I know, crazy to be bandying around Freud with one of his estimable practitioners. A little reading goes a long way to being a lot dangerous eh?

Perhaps you'd go so far as to say my reading fixation makes me one of civilisation's discontents? Not in the least actually. See books may well disappoint, may let you down, but they never betray you. The good ones can shine a light inside, reflect your secrets back to you. But they never go outside the borders of the room in which you share such revelation. Now I know you have the equivalent privacy of analysand and analyst, that you would never disclose anything divulged in this room and that even, perish the thought, were I to become a case study it would be anonymised. Therefore it cannot ever be a question of betrayal with you. But have you the same ability to shine a light into the lesser exhibited parts of my psyche? Since that's what you're up against. That is the benchmark for you and your couch here.

However, I am fully conscious of the limitations of restricting one's understanding to just the printed word. How could I possibly assimilate the full extent of Freud's wisdom, without exposing myself to undergo the transference process? That's why I'm here lying horizontally, ninety degrees from the reading position. Trying out a talking cure rather than a written one. Although for a talking cure you certainly don't say a lot. There's somewhat of a dearth of dialogue being transacted here and now. A bit of diegesis from you now and again would most certainly be welcomed. However, it's me doing most of the actual talking. Monologuing. I can get that all day and every day at home on my own. That's another plus about books. They let me hear other voices than my own. They cause the sound of my own voice to die down for the duration. Held rapt and stilled, through listening to the words of others.

Don't you find the body of psychoanalytic knowledge

shares much in common with that of fiction? No hear me out. Your whole corpus is built is it not, on the back of a story? Oedipus and Electra. And I know I take my life in my hands talking to a Freudian about Carl Jung, but his whole framework was erected on myth and communally held narratives. Oh come off it, what is a case study but the *story* of one psyche? A memoir slewed for the psychoanalytical diagnostic points. Third person omniscient narrator. That's you the analyst. While the analysand sits, lies here, relating their story, albeit out of sequence and in a non-linear associative order informed by the emotions behind it. If you'll excuse me for presuming to tell you your job, but you'll be looking to restore the linearity, make the emotions all flow and drive towards a redeeming denouement. A good author needs a good editor. No as a Freudian you'll like this. The only thing collective about our species is our symbolic and linguistic systems. Hard wired grammatical facility. But given how limited they are, confined by our perceptual and sensing apparatus, it's hardly surprising that the output they produce, our so-called stories, themselves don't show much range or variation. Now to Jung, that seemed to mean a collective unconscious, but any common or garden novelist today will tell you there are only six or seven plots they have to work with. That speaks to a lack of creative imagination to come up with any more than that.

Before you cavil, consider this. In fiction people go on journeys. Learning pilgrimages from their own experiences and events in the course of the book. They are very changed beasts from that which they were at the book's start. Yet let's face it, real life just isn't like that. People are stuck in their behaviour. They repeat the same mistakes, inhabit the same reflexive, or seemingly reflexive frameworks of response as they always do. You have to concur with that, for it is such stuckness and immobility that brings people to your consulting room here in the first place is it not? They are frozen in some childhood stage of maldevelopment which determines so much of their adult behaviour. Yes, me included. I won't deny that. So your job is to unplug the blockage. I know, I chose my term deliberately. To take me on a journey, from childhood emotional paralysis, into the wide-open world of adulthood. To reknit aspects of my story together to throw up new insights and to reorder them for the future. Thus we begin to approximate the plot of a novel. Ergo why should I not just stick to reading my books? What am I paying you for? 'A good author needs a good editor'? Oh touché, well played sir.

Reading's too passive? Actually I would offer the converse. That I am highly active when I enflesh the characters I am reading about. I reflect and refract them back to my life. To see how we differ and what we share in common. Whether I can take aspects of them to myself, to wear parts of them like a skin. Yes, that's the oral phase referenced now, in addition to the anal we've already ticked. The Oedipal? Assuredly I tucked that one away as successfully resolved, being neither in love with my mother, nor threatened by my father, at quite an early age. It was never about sexual desire for me. Yes, could we park that and return to it at a later date? I'm pursuing a thread here I'd like to persist with. No, I think you'll find it enlightening. Yes sorry, that was a bit presumptuous. But please, if we could just stick with this for a few more moments? Thank you. The fear I have of being cured, is that I'll lose the books themselves. That if you were to kick away the stacked pit props of volumes, the whole mine shaft will cave in and overwhelm my mind exposed to the daylight. Yes like Samson and the Philistines. The only worthwhile tale in the Bible to my mind, though I suppose you headshrinkers rather favour Jonah emerging from the belly of the beast back into the light from his submerged unconscious. I've always wondered why Sigmund plumped for a cautionary tale from the Ancient Classic canon, when there are so many manifestations of father-son rivalry in the OT; Adam and Eve defying God the father; God ordering Abraham to kill his son Isaac; Jacob fooling his blind father to get a birthright. Samson being blind and also castrated by Delilah getting him to cut his hair off. Did you know that the word 'testament' comes from the root of 'testes'? That veracity was sworn by cupping the old crown jewels, bearing witness to one's masculinity. How's that for the phallic phase upon which a whole culture was erected? Oh, you did know.

Anyway, we digress. Sorry yes, I'm digressing. Sublimation isn't it called, oh no wait that's the other one. This is an ironclad case of displacement isn't it? Oh I had it right first time, did I? And projection too I'd wager, because like I say, it is an exerted act on my part. To return to the point at hand. I fear that weaning me off books might be like an amputation. The loss of some valuable, vital part of my psyche, never to regain it? That's scary. What will come in its stead? Books made me the person I am, and I quite like the vast majority of him. What, you think reading actually shrouds the person I am? See this is the thing I'm confused about. Supposedly maladjusted folk come here, Freud's discontents muzzled by societal norms, and you free them up from their suppressed furies to what purpose? As Freud himself says, to have them fit into a properly determined society full of rules of propriety. The triumph of the superego regulating our actions within decent bounds. But at what cost? The artists and cultural pioneers of our society don't fit into nice tramlines of thought and being. I credit that society and people lose so much with this cure you proffer. I might just sacrifice the things about me that are worth being me for. I know it's an irrational concern really. But that makes it no less real right? My parents both seemed perfectly content for their son to be a bookworm. No, don't worry, you can't possibly represent either mum or dad taking my books away from me, because it never happened. Neither of them ever tried to stop me reading. Why on earth would they? I was never a problem to them. Caused them absolutely no anxiety whatsoever. Yes, I suppose the worm is a lowly, legless phallic animal. Blind too.

You know I think Papa Freud missed out a stage or two after the resolution of the Oedipal conflict phase. For example, what of the reading phase? Particularly germane to my case of course. Bolstering the superego through seeing how others view and contribute towards enshrining it. Why not, the brain is an erogenous zone? It facilitates a great source of pleasure, or at least mine does. There's a whole school of literary criticism based on psychoanalytical readings of texts. Can't say I'm an adherent of it myself, but it's out there, well established and mused on in august academic institutions. No I didn't. Can you imagine me at college? Precisely. Anyway, what do you think of my theory? Perhaps I got stuck at this phase and never managed to break on through it into full maturity. Why not, Lacan argued for a mirror stage for infants that Freud never made mention of? Yes, I know, more dangerous reading around our mutual subject. Which is quite funny really, seeing as Lacan's mirror stage is all about representing the gateway for the switch from subjectivity and self-involvement, into beginning to locate oneself in part of a bigger society outside wouldn't you say? No of course you wouldn't. He's a threat after all. A competitor. A rival analytical school. Not in the original French, no. Sadly. The greatest regret from my childhood, that I didn't pay more heed to studying modern languages. I would have liked to have learned German, French and Russian, languages of the great literary works. Spanish not so much, "DQ" aside. For the nuance of course, surely you as an analyst, can appreciate the value of the shades of meaning behind words? I mean you practically founded a whole practise upon it. Or should that be 'praxis'? As in parapraxis. Am I always like this in my dealings with people? I don't know, you're the only person I rub up against, so I have nothing to compare it with. The statistical sample is insufficient. Do I think I'm using you to blow off steam, like a pent up saucepan on the boil? Like a what, a scratching post you mean? I'm not being aggressive I'll have you know. The very act of distancing implied by a simile, means it can hardly be aggressive now can it? Oh I see, it's not a bad thing. Shows there's hope for me then, ha I like that!

No I wouldn't say I had a mania for reading. I'm not a febrile reader, more considered and sedate. Anyway, it's a loaded word that. You have to ask? Why 'mania' of course. You head doctors are very quick at labelling people. I'm with RD Laing that madness is socially constructed and defined. Though I wouldn't have let all the nutters out of the sanatoriums straight off the bat. First you need to-look who I'm trying to teach to suck eggs! No, rather than a mania, I might describe it as more of a cacoethes. Oh you're not familiar with the word? Not a classical education then. Me neither. Autodidact, courtesy of, well, reading. Cacoethes also means mania, but the shade of difference is in the suffix, from the etymology of 'ethos', as in rather than madness, it's an ethos, an attitude of mind. And yes 'caco-' means 'bad', but it has no etymological links to ca-ca which I'm sure you shrinks are fully familiar with as the cherished prime constituent of the anal phase. No, I'm not well versed in being insulting at all, how could I be? I don't come up against anyone to insult. It's all just words after all. Words from books, worked on and transmuted by my grey matter. Maybe that exact same sequence of words came from something I read but long forgotten as to its source? What? Yes, perhaps every single possible combination of words has already been put together and there is nothing new to say. But then I haven't read every book ever written yet. Yes, even this very exchange we're having, might already exist in some book somewhere. And it certainly will be if you make me into a case study. How does that make me feel? No, far from recycled, or vicarious. I feel... condoned. I know it is a strange word, but if I'd said 'absolved' or 'pardoned' they are too fraught with associations and meanings. Too Oedipal.

I think I made a breakthrough this week. I was in my kitchen preparing a meal for supper and I was suddenly struck by a thought about the novel I had just finished reading prior to dinner. But instead of breaking off from shredding the vegetables to go back and refer directly to the source of the book itself, I picked up my mobile phone from the countertop and went online to pursue my inquiries. How about that for a change of behaviour? Not bad hey? Really, that's the angle you're taking on it? What use I have for a mobile phone? No I don't use it to ring people, as I'm led to believe with most citizens these days, a phone is used for anything but making calls. Well I've told you, I mainly use it to do my online shopping. But now I suppose I've opened a Pandora's Box- no smutty associations please- to a whole welter of online discussion and debate on literature. It's called the virtual world after all isn't it? No, don't worry, I have no intention of letting this resource feed and stiffen my compulsiveness. Oh, and the other thing I use my phone for is to record these sessions. Ah, I didn't realise you weren't aware I did that. I find it very… helpful. I go home and transcribe our exchange, well hardly an exchange in reality and preserve the record for review. Just like you do the same I'm sure. What, yes I suppose it does replicate the mechanisms we're trying to work me away from. Oh well. Baby steps.

I think I suffered somewhat of a setback today. Not so much perhaps, that you'd confer on it the status of a regression. You know my phone? Well I was unavoidably walking along the street to the postbox to return some official form you inexplicably cannot complete online and I admit I was consulting some literary gloss, which meant I didn't see the man come up to me. Whereupon he hit me and stole my phone. That would never happen with books. It might happen in a book, but never when you're locked up nice and safe within the four walls of your fortress, book in hand. But yes, a salutary lesson today. Encapsulates the whole reason I'm here, still can't break me of my reading habit. Well maybe verging on an obsession more than a habit yes. Who? I don't know. A shadowy figure that's all. A man without a face. A skull recessed behind his hood. Yes, very evocative. Where are you going with this? He doesn't represent anything to me. You're curious as to why I refuse to entertain encounters with strangers in real life, but am content enough to embrace the strangers in books and the strangers who pen them? I hadn't thought of that before. Made the connection... Well, part of the difference is the function of time. I can go at my own pace with a book. Sit back. Reflect. Muse. The same is simply not possible in the world of people. Snap judgements. Of books by their cover, people by their physiognomies. Social intercourse policing the intervals of communication exchange. Why are we still banging on down this road? You seem a bit obsessed- hey, it wasn't you was it? The man in the hood. Can't break me of my book habit through a talking cure, so adopts a more direct method of action? No of course not. I hardly see you in a hooded sweatshirt. Not over your suit and tie. Paranoid? No, not in the slightest. I am many things, but don't add that to the list. Never had cause for it before, because I don't interact with other people, so where's the potential for paranoia? Let's chalk it down... (or is it up?)... to transference. There, that's a good sign, right? That you're looming up... that you're entering my calculations of the everyday. Yes, granted, a tad negative in this particular instance. Hardly persecutory though. Apart from the inconvenience of a trip down to the mobile phone shop and the inevitably disagreeable persiflage there, the robber did me a favour. Snapped me right out of a bad habit, before it had fledged into a full compulsion. I acknowledge that this is a foundation stone. A chink, a ray of light. If I can relate to you, then it augurs well for the formation of future relationships. Isn't that the trajectory it's supposed to follow? Oh I see. How can we still be at the exposition stage? You do realise of course that one 'relates' a story... No I do not live my whole life in 'speech marks'!

I can't help feeling we need to jump start the process a bit. Move us along to the meaty stuff. The nitty gritty.

So I'll revisit my delayed promise of how I resolved my Oedipal stage to help us along. What, you'll be the judge of that? Very good. It's taken eight months or so, but we finally got you to crack a joke. Oh confound it all man! Don't give me all that it's the analytical method and that's only my interpretation. I'm adjudging it to be a joke on your part. Because you're warming to me. No my father didn't crack jokes. He was an utterly humourless man. I know what you're trying to do here. But I won't let you sidetrack me. This is my version of the Oedipal stage and it's really rather simple. I always skip over the raunchy parts in novels. No stay with me here. I simply am not interested in such tawdry descriptions. And while I perceive that there could be some development of character or relationship seeping through the juxtaposition of anatomies in the act of coitus, I find, or rather found, the descriptive language veered between the leaden and the fanciful. Often within the same sentence, therefore utterly noisome and undermined anything that could be so gleaned. A right royally risible mélange of the anatomical and the metaphorical. Talk about regression, even the noble author seems to revert to the infantile when essaying to wield his tool of semantics to meet the carnal. No matter the name of the author on the book's spine, still the sniggering emerges from behind the po-faced phrases he tries to employ in these sections of his work. Never at any stage did such episodes engage my curiosity, including when I was a child. Rather I was grateful, since all the energy that supposedly accumulates in the genital area, has in my case incontestably diverted away and on up to my brain. To help the reading drive. Upped my daily page rate. Sex is beyond language, therefore it is of no interest to me. So you see there never was any issue of lusting after my mother, fearing the jealousy of my father and not one second was given to any consideration of the putative fall of the axe down over my chap. No, I'm not claiming I'm smarter than everybody else. We're just talking about how one marshals one's resources. I'm talking only in terms of the energy devoted to a task. You must appreciate that. Freud's theories hinged on biological notions of energies and blockages. Well alright, early Freud yes. What do you mean maybe I might be better off with acupuncture? How's that going to cure me of compulsive novel reading? Although the holistic approach of the needles, to rebalance the energy flows around the body, is not dissimilar to the flow of a narrative…

My final session today. No I'm fine about it honestly. Not a single pang of separation anxiety. One chapter closes and another one- Yes, right, sure. Of course. To sum up what have I learned about myself? I know reading instructs me in nothing relating to real life. However, what I do learn from it, is all about the nature of fiction itself. Which probably means I can see my own delusions for what they are. Deals I make with myself, with my psyche, in order to retain an even keel. So I can exist perennially in the world of books, rather than within the physical world my body is lodged in and not suffer any distress from it. How would that hermetic world become threatened? I can't conceive of a circumstance. By a book that pulls away all the preconceptions of fiction? A place where stories no longer stack up? I've read the Modernists, the experimentalists and the metafictionists and I don't believe there's any such book with that kind of iconoclastic power. But I'll drop you a line from my rubber room if ever I come across one and it brings down the bookstack towers of my Jericho.

The Eighteenth Brumaire of Péter Sclemihl

Once upon a time ad infinitum.

Once upon a time ad nauseam. Since it is important to encrypt the key archetypes; echo sustain the reverberating symbols; taxiderm the tendentious tropes; and conserve the constant conjunctures. There is much conjecture as to how much degeneration occurred from the oral tradition, once it was set down on the page and ramrodded into the literary canon. But nothing compared to the twenty and twenty-first century mutation of the morals such tales were supposed to inculcate. Besides, contemporary children's imaginations are scarce populated with denizens from the faerie realm. Magic and transformation these days take place courtesy of fibre optics, usually through a gunsight and lots of pixelated cruor.

So…

Once upon a time in the here and now. Did the oral fabulists really start their story-spinning thus? Or was it a superimposition wrought by the literary trans cribbers? It is not insignificant that the Brothers Grimm, stewards of the first from-the-horse's-mouth volume of fairy tales, hailed from Germany? The country that presided over Max Weber, he who laid bare the nature of all bureaucracy and bureaucratic processes and tied it up with red tape ribbon on the top. Additionally, also the culture whence Franz Kafka could acutely lance that very same boil through literature:

"Als Gregor Samsa eines Morgens aus unruhigen Träumen erwachte, fand er sich in seinem Bett zu einem ungeheueren Ungeziefer verwandelt."

Note, not once upon a time, but 'one morning'. One particular specified point in the space-time continuum, rather than some airy-FAIRY finger wagged in the embers of dying orality (down Sigmund, not your cue yet). That is, such fantastical transformation happened irrevocably just the once. There was to be no recurrent climbing out of the wolf's digestive tract. No princes reverting from frogs' metamorphoses. No moral flip-flopping about to facilitate good triumphing over evil.

Now giant bug conversions and subsequent grievous wounding by an Oedipally-discarded apple core is exactly what I would dub a 'fairy tale'. But that's a whole other story. Or even the neologistic old chestnut 'genre'. We aren't dealing with far and away tales here my campfire marshmallow roasting confreres. We dare to deal in woah! stories. Wary stories. More briquettes on the barbie please Jaroslav. And Max, don't let Franz throw his jottings on the flames this time. Plays merry hell with the flavour.

The slain-giant of this, my unsanitary salutary tale, derives from the same stirps as tubercular Franz. Originally (once upon a time) a Piotr or Petr, but Anglicised to Peter, which in an affectation of the newly adult, he himself appended an acute accent. Letter changes to and from father and son. In some ways, this tale too is a letter to the father, but this one shall be signed-sealed-delivered rather than wimped out on. Consumer and consumptive derive from the same etymological root. Etymology is not to be confused with entomology, which is where Franz's bug can be taxonomied. Franz worked in insurance, not taxation and revenue. Did Newton make a mint from the Mint he superintended? Idle hands make for the Devil's work.

Oh dear with all this structuralist meandering, we don't seem to have ascended terribly far from the "once upon a time" launch pad. Reality's gravitational pull seems forever wanting to haul nary fairy-teller me back down to earth. Einstein worked neither in revenue nor insurance, but in patents. Isaac and Albert, bureaucrats each, yet with such fiendishly creative minds. They challenged the data of their senses. Not much utility in fairy tale flights of fancy for them then. Mind you, gedankenexperiment...

Fairy stories largely originated within feudal agrarianism, whereby they overtly immersed many of their characters in poverty. Cinderella as a serf to her sisters; Hansel and Gretel living in a time of rural famine and being abandoned accordingly; Jack and the Beanstalk where the family are down to their last asset in the shape of a milch cow. Magick kicks in to enable them all to escape their penurious circumstances, culminating in marrying into royalty or finding the golden egg. Magic in place of the modern-day sorcery of agents, PR's & kiss and tell newspaper deals. A supernatural gloss applied to a poorly comprehended mechanism of the market, swapping a cow for some beans for example, representing a cockeyed rate of exchange. Other cultures' folklore are full of merchants and even some proto-bourgeois folk, but we're here subsumed within the Western European tradition. If we are to update them, then we must contextualise them with due regard. Just sayin'.

Once upon a time in late stage capitalism (late as in lingeringly tardy rather than demise, more's the pity), there lived a man. Péter Sch- was a very successful parasite upon the bloated carcass of society. The apex panderer-predator. A superstructural solicit-or, hegemonic gate-keeper to the secret relationships of the material base masked behind law. This jumped-up lad from Manor House, London E.13, lived in a huge, nay bloated manor house, in the anachronistic manner of a squire. Said house wasn't fabricated from gingerbread nor chocolate, though it did have gold taps in the bathroom. The cutlery was gold too and as an unremitting meat eater, admittedly cooked rather than raw, my how he liked to see that blood red juice run from his chops. No veg, no fresh fruit. Save from apples wedged in the mouth of spit-roasted suckling pig. But these Cox'ses had to be bought in, since though this had once been a Medieval orchard, he'd had all the trees levelled in order to construct his citydwell in the countryside. As was the fashion in loutish Loughton, land of the churls, near the decidedly unenchanted Epping Forest.

Another facet of fairy tales is the motif of family. Ugly sisters, cruel, neglectful parents, godmothers and grandparents. Many failed families with step-relations, though this could actually reflect early age mortality and remarriage in an age of disease, malnutrition and death in childbirth, rather than today's contemporary malaise of disposability. The fissile nuclear family in meltdown. Whatever the root and branch cause, a signal dialectic of oppressors and liberators.

So this family had all the trappings. Sch-'s wife was caparisoned with her horse. Not though in a Tsarina Catherine The Great way you understand, for there is no place for urban myths in a fairy story. Besides, there might be children reading (unlikely as that is). Nothing remotely tacky in this manor house's tack room. While his daughter was in receipt of tennis lessons from a dashing coach. But there was no undue double faulting to be had there either, since she was to remain unseeded throughout her life (though perhaps not virginal). Crosscourt backhanding her coach's forlornly lobbed compliments away, she never yielded her baseline. Defensiveness became muscle memory. Me, I had a pot-bellied pig for my mute chaperon through the kingdom. I loved that pig (the porcine one rather than the human, though the likeness was uncanny. The jowls, I think). No magic beans, pig in a poke barter from me. I was commodity fetishised wedded to my porker. Hey, no sniggering at the back there.

Absolutely not, for if there was any barnstorming libidinous behaviour on show at all, it was laid solely at the door of my father and well away from the environs of home. A mobile, boundaryless rite de seigneur. There were no ricks here. The only magic, the only thing fantastical about this whole lairy story, is how a man so ugly as to rank a veritable ogre, pulled such a G-string of beautiful women. Money buys you a lot of pull I guess. That is one of the (a-)morals of this grimy tale. Actually thinking about it, perhaps it's when Western Europe entered a cash nexus economy, that sparked the need to transcribe what had formerly only existed as oral transmissions. When it no longer remains preserved for free by the hearth, or subject to the vagaries of negotiation and barter with a wandering minstrel, but rather set down on the printed page for a fixed price. Arggh, my fairy story barely even rates as a story, for all this dialectical materialist critique. Back to the hegemonic discourse.

There comes a time (a sustained periodicity, not a one-off, nor a vague atemporal 'once'), when consumer capitalism consumes itself. Granting no further surplus value to be squeezed from the flayed meat picked clean from its corpus. When the illicit affairs carry no sexual charge. When the gourmandising no longer excites the jaded palate. When the copious alcoholic necking fails to intoxicate the senses. Even his propensity for successfully playing the odds, for wagering on horses, cards, equities, future commodities (holes in the ground for the foundation stones of castles in the air), for staking money in order to yield a greater return on that money, speculative specious specie, has all gone to the dogs. Like the dope fiend, increasing tolerance compels yet more potent dosages just to attain the same level, which of course in itself is ultimately unsatisfying, since the craving demands only an ever-escalating pleasure. This represents the true moral of this tale, an absolute paradigmatic symbology, but doubtless the hegemonic mutability will reabsorb it and spit out some closing cloying homily with which to leave the opiated reader. Boy the Ancient Greeks sold us a pup with catharsis. It lets the audience off the hook, their stirred insurgent emotions assuaged by the purgative action of the text. Bequeathing only the possibility of an anorexic cadre. A vanguard so emaciated, that you can simultaneously see their front and back sides on the same vertical plane. Without having to travel anywhere near the speed of light.

So Péter Sch- attained the stage where the ante finally ups sticks and resumes the long march of the antegrade of history. He contracts an STD. He also loses the appreciation of sweet things upon his palate and becomes increasingly bitter at its desertion, particularly in regard to his horrifically calorifically toothsome desserts. He becomes incontinent, whereupon the instant a drop of ethanol passes the frontier of his throat, the much put-upon border guards in the bladder mulct their toll. And finally, he was having to buy-in increasing entry stakes, as the permutations all clicked against him. The parlous parlays entailed longer and longer shots to make good his losses, but they inevitably came up all too-probably short. Long and short of it, he wasn't left with a pot to incontinently piss in. So he embezzled money from his clients, creaming off their court payouts. He readily laundered the readies from his law firm. This petty chiseler raided the petty cash without leaving any receipt chits. And of course, being a gambler down on his luck, the whole house of cards blew in on him like a wolf outside a piggy's home fabricated from straw. The bricks and mortar of Manor House were under threat of repossession, though he'd concealed the fact from his family. But there came a time when his law firm caught him with his hand in the cookie jar, concomitant with the Law Society beginning proceedings to strike him off their rolls. Pawnbroker and porn-broker alike failed to assist him halt his alarming slide as he hit rock bottoms up (so much for customer care and loyalty card entry to high stakes card tables). There was only one praxis remaining, a certain self-decentralisation. A withering away of the troubled state of Péter Sch–.

He took a carving knife to his arteries while recumbent in the tub. Not without first sozzling and sousing his miserable spirit in whisky. A cocktail of Dutch Courage, scotch mist and marinaded trousers. Thereby inhibiting the body's inhibitors. Refluxing the reflexes of innate self-preservation. Anyhoo, he opened his wrists up. Venesected his venal venom. Phlebotomised his er flagging phlogiston? ... The blood bubbled like a seething cauldron's brew. The sap spurted like biting into a poisoned Pink Lady (heightened language = heightened awareness, employing Brechtian alienation technique):

FAIRY TALE CHECKBOX

APPLE	YES [x]	NO [ ]
FOREST	YES [x]	NO [ ]
ANIMAL GUIDE	YES [x]	NO [ ]
OGRE	YES [x]	NO [ ]
FAIRY GODMOTHER	YES [½]	NO [ ]

The source of red denial. Blood is blood. No matter how many juicy or maggoty apples you bite into.

Mamma in her mourning glory, felt that her presently dyed chestnut thatch (to match the sorrel equine she had recently taken delivery of, albeit unaware that it had been purchased on the never never), might appear a bit too vivid for a funeral and resolved to de-lustre. She stood hunched over the bathroom porcelain, gold taps spouting a gush of water, unbeknownst to her in eerie echo of the spurt from her ex-husband's veins (fortunately the maid had agreed to wash out the bath, in return for an increased stipend. Hey, that's the let-the-blood-run-free-market for you). She bent her head beneath the cataract and the dye began to sluice. It pooled and flowed and abstract arted, its rich copper tint diluted by the water into a blood-red hue. There was more than a hint of the Lady

Macbeth about this, even though she had whispered no exhortations, nor poured any poisons into the ear of her decedent husband. Typical of the misogyny of the fairy tale world, of washing a man right out of your hair, that such an association could even be drawn. (Thanks Mr Bettleheim sir. Oh and Sigmund's called you out by the way. Reckons you stole his walk on part. See you in court). But there again, we've got the notion of hair dye, of human transformation, of changing yourself into something other and then washing it clean and purified back to the original essence. If the exegesis is longer than the original metaphor itself, then we're inelegantly fabling. Apologue-ies.

My sister, well she was too busy out on the court practising her two-handed drop shot with topspin slice, to attend the funeral service. Live and let.

For my part, I lustrated. Rolled in my father's blood. Smeared myself in it like a pig in mud. Got my pot-bellied to do the same to enflesh the metaphor. There's a 'dictatorship of the p-roll-etariat' cached somewhere within that, but the revolution waits for no man, so we lack for the time to unearth its pun-iterative truffle. I had completely blood glazed my own skin. Now we're talking all-e-gory. This is what I call a fairy tale ending. Unfortunately it's one of those false (consciousness) endings. There's a bit more business to transact yet. Soz.

The sole shame of it was that it had not been spilled at my hand, but at his own. Still, I revelled in its metallic stickiness. Its tensile blobbiness. The troll is no more. Ding-dong (is that a siren in the distance?) the witch (sociopath in today's psychobabble parlance) is snuffed. Rejoice. The tin despotism is over. Canned. No more tyranny of walking on eggshells (are eggshells an established fairy story emblem? Why not?) Our estate is free, withered away, the villagers – if we had any – would no longer toil under an autocracy. As evidenced already by the maid van-not-so-guardedly flexing her increased muscle in the labour market.

WITCH YES [x] NO [ ]

Sure we might struggle without his formerly plenteous income. We may even starve, though I reckon my pot-bellied porker would keep us going for a while. (See, where are the magic beans when you really need them for an unequal trade? Who's the schlemihl now, oh I guess under the law of patrimony it's me). But no more do we labour under the burden of maintaining this falsification. No more will our forearms be bruised and sprained as we reach out to stop him tumbling. No longer will we have to flip him back over into the fray. This festering domestic vesicle can now be lanced for all its pus to drain. The magic spell over this gilded bricks and mortar has finally been lifted like a bad curse. The misfortune brought about by an amassed fortune.

CURSE YES [x] NO [ ]

Now you can see us for what we are. Tired and cracked and worn and scratched and threadbare and hollow and haunted and abused. In other words, capitalised.

This is the story of my struggle.

A fare thee badly tale. With an unhappy ending.

It is of course the ultimate sacrilege of the folk tale art. For we all know there is no first-person singular narration. A Bonapartism of the worst sort. 'I' wants no part in it.

"The first as tragedy, then as farce."

"Das eine Mal als Tragödie, das andere Mal als Farce."
So there's no flaming 'once upon a time' about it.

Twice upon a time…

Raised by Wolves

Guess who's just sold his book to a publisher! Yes, isn't it just? Of course, I couldn't have done it without you darling – I did dedicate the thing to you. A two book deal. So Nathan, I'll dedicate the next one in your name. No, I have no idea what the follow-up will be yet. First things first, eh? Let's just bask in the glory of this one, shall we? We should crack open a bottle to toast to its success. And a Fruit Shoot for the lad. What does 'dedicate' mean? Well, it means that the book is especially written for you. Absolutely you can read it. But I think you'll find it a bit long to read just at the moment. Yes thank you Sheilagh dear, I'm quite aware of your contribution as I've already acknowledged. Maybe when you're a bit older Nat. It will be a nice thing to come to. Shame we've no booze in the house to celebrate. Yes, you can still have the Fruit Shoot son.

My agent was amazing. A real terrier. And a terror. You should have seen her in action. Feeding them exactly what they wanted to hear. Spinning my book so much so

I almost didn't recognise it as mine. Clever old boot. Yes, almost as changed as after my editor had gone through it. And yet still not as many words as you pruned Sheilagh dear. It was too. But yes, I'll own you improved it. Not beyond recognition, no. Okay buddy, enjoy your programme, make sure you don't rub it off when you've finished watching, because you'll want to keep it to watch again.

The agent says it's now the hard work starts. I've got to provide copy for the blurb, my author biog, the website. No darling of course I shouldn't have to be sullying my hands with all that sort of hocus-pocus. I'm an artiste after all. It's official too now. Yes, I was being ironic. I haven't the first idea for any of them. The biog, well I think I can handle that. But a blurb? I thought the marketing department did that sort of thing. I mean if I could have shrunk the story down to a blurb, I wouldn't have needed to write all those words in the first place would I? I could have just summed it up in a couple of paras. Well yes, perhaps. Actually that's not a bad idea. I wonder if I even kept the submission letter I sent her? Mind you, that was more of a full treatment than a blurb. But it's a start. Helps shiver down the number of words. And a website? That's a laugh. Somehow have to keep feeding it content like a minotaur. What? That's not funny Sheilagh. Unless you kept all the sections you removed for me, cos sure as hell I don't still have them. What, yes sorry Nathan! Didn't know you'd come back in the kitchen.

Who would have thought that with our one simple story, Daddy would become a professional author? You inspired me Nathan. All those things we do together. The places we go like Nursery. Actually Sheilagh, I do a little more than just stand around with the few other dads bitching about all the women in the car park. We cut that section anyway. Or football training or storytime at the library. Or especially the changing rooms at the swimming pool, the funny little things you pick up in there. No it didn't sound wrong Sheilagh. Not to my ears. Yep, turns out there's money in that there childrearing. I know you're off earning serious money in the world of the grown-ups Sheilagh, but the stay at home dad's forays out into the child's world has turned out to be reasonably lucrative too don't you think? Put us on the map. Now we can probably afford to move to a nicer map. You know you can fast forward through the adverts Nat? There's a clever boy. Well yes we live in a satnav world, the map is metaphorical as you well know.

Hey, I still had to take all those anecdotes and funny experiences and turn them into a coherent book. And create a believable character. The heck you did! It did not need wholesale knocking into shape. He certainly didn't need any rough burs smoothed out. Is that how you see me? No, of course not. The main character isn't me. Only loosely based. And the kid definitely isn't Nat. I wouldn't use him like that. Expose him for all the world to see. Well if you felt like that Sheilagh, why did you show such support for it? Why did you pour all that labour into it? It's a bit flipping late for that now isn't it? Well which bits? Not that it's going to make any difference now anyway. It's all finalised, ready for typesetting. Really? That passage? You don't know what you're talking about. That's one of the best passages of my writing. What else? You're on more solid ground with that one, the editor chucked it out. Yeah and that section. Look, alright you made your point. Maybe I should have asked you which bits you'd keep in. No, don't answer that. I know where this ends. Your version would be the elevator pitch. The one line summary that tells the whole story. That's because we're different you and I. Prolix? No, I meant we have different dreams that's all. And now I finally got the chance to pursue mine. No of course it wasn't Nat getting in the way of it. If anything he's totally facilitated it. No, that does not mean I'm exploiting- this is not off the back of him. This was my blood, sweat and tears. None of that could be said to be the same when looking after Nat, since that was a pleasure. Is – is an absolute pleasure. Yeah, a labour of love. Twin labours of love. Non-identical. Not the same things at all. Different parts of me. Different emotions. You can't be around a child, surrounded by children all day, without any adult company and not go a bit crackers. So this was an important release. To restore equilibrium. It helped keep me balanced. Makes me a better father. Well I credit that it does. Yes of course I'll put some of my advance in his savings account. The one I had the foresight to set up originally if you remember?

I know what this is. This is your jealousy coming out. You would take away my success. Now you've had your eyes opened that your work isn't quite as fulfilling as mine. How am I going to write a follow-up when we've no more children to plunder? Totally below the belt Sheilagh. No I am not stealing anything from Nat. Not even borrowing from his life. Nat is not the story. Any more than I'm the story. We're not living life as stories and anecdotes. Well yes, the parents swap anecdotes because there's not much else happening in our lives other than childrearing. We exchange tips as well, but I'm not going to write a self-help book now, am I? God help me, it's never been about that. We haven't changed anything or any activity that we've done, or how we do it, just with the book in mind. He is not my 'guinea pig'… He is my son. And I love him. He can read this in years to come and look back and recollect elements of his childhood. But not in any one-to-one direct correspondence. I've worked this…. there's no other word for it, material. More than just changed the names and places. It has to appeal to lots of people. The agent and publishers certainly seem to think it does. It will. And that's because I've shaped it. Like a sculptor does with his clay. Yes of course it's fictionalised. What did you imagine it was going to be categorised as, memoir? It's all true and none of it is true. But there has to be a grain of truth in each event for it to be believable. For it to ring authentically.

A conversation that never happened. The book I never wrote. A life I never lived. The son I never had. A father I never was. Fiction.

About the Author

Born in 1964, Marc Nash is the author of six novels. His previous novel, *Three Dreams in the Key of G*, was shortlisted for the Not the Booker Prize in 2018. He works as a finance director for a charity and lives in London.